TRAPPED

and *Liberated*

THE PRIVATEER'S BOLD BELOVED

BY
BREE WOLF

This is a work of fiction. Names, characters, businesses, places, brands, media, events and incidents are either the products of the author's imagination or used in a fictitious manner.

Any resemblance to actual persons, living or dead, or actual events is purely coincidental.

Cover Art by Victoria Cooper
Copyright © 2018 Bree Wolf

Paperback ISBN: 978-3-96482-034-1
Hardcover ISBN: 978-3-96482-121-8

www.breewolf.com

All Rights Reserved

To my Devoted Readers
Shauna Joesten
Eris Hyrkas
Debbie Clatterbuck
Kaye Gunter
Gina Johnson
May You Never Leave Me

Acknowledgments

My thank-you to all of you who've helped with feedback, typo detection, character and plot development, editing, formatting, cover creation, and the biggie...spreading the word...so that countless readers can now enjoy these stories of love's second chance.

To name only a few: Michelle Chenoweth, Monique Taken, Zan-Mari Kiousi, Tray-Ci Roberts, Kim Bougher, Vicki Goodwin, Denise Boutin, Elizabeth Greenwood, Corinne Lehmann, Lynn Herron, Karen Semones, Maria DB, Kim O'Shea, Tricia Toney, Deborah Montiero, Keti Vezzu, Patty Michinko, Lynn Smith, Vera Mallard, Isabella Nanni, Carol Bisig, Susan Czaja, Teri Donaldson, Anna Jimenez and Tammy Windsor.

An additional thank you goes to Marie-Andrée Gignac, who read through all those French expressions uttered by Antoine and Henri, making certain they're...well, actual French expressions.

TRAPPED
and
Liberated

Prologue

England 1777 (or a variation thereof)

"Good night, Sweetheart."

Smiling at her mother, Alexandra Sombersby snuggled into her pillows, enjoying the softness of her little cocoon as she closed her eyes. Dimly, she heard the door close and her mother's footsteps walk down the small corridor until their sounds were swallowed up by the soft howling of the wind outside her window.

Even at the young age of six, Alexandra knew that she was one of the few fortunate children of her station. One of the few who was tucked in at night not by a nanny or governess, but by her own mother. Although Miss Barton, their governess, kept a sharp eye on Alexandra and her elder brother during the day, bedtime was a moment that belonged to Alexandra and her mother alone.

Huddled together in Alexandra's bed, the two of them would pull up the coverlet, enjoying the warmth of their embrace, and her mother would tell her a story.

A fairy tale.

A tale of beautiful princesses, of knights in shining armour, of evil dragons and long journeys that always, always led to a happily-ever-after.

Her mother's soothing voice would chase away the excitement of the day and gently lull her to sleep. Often, Alexandra was not awake to bid her mother a good night. Often, she slipped into a deep and peaceful slumber before her mother had even whispered the words, "And they lived happily ever after."

Alexandra loved nothing more but these quiet moments alone with her mother. They were her favourite part of the day, and yet, she longed for the moment when she would be all grown up, find her own Prince Charming and live happily-ever-after.

What would he be like? Alexandra mused as her eyelids fluttered closed and a large yawn pulled on her lips. Naturally, there was no need for him to save her from a tower. Would she meet him at a ball then? Or by chance when walking about the countryside?

Alexandra sighed, picturing all the different ways her own Prince Charming might sweep her off her feet and carry her off to his castle.

If only that moment was not that far off. If only she did not have to wait so much longer.

Still, what mattered was that he would find her.

After all, there was someone destined for her out there, was there not?

In the depth of her little heart, Alexandra believed that there was, and when sleep claimed her, her dreams put a gentle smile on her little face.

Chapter One

DREAMS COME TRUE

London 1789

Twelve years later

Alexandra Sombersby felt her legs tremble as she slowly walked into the grand ballroom on her father's arm. Her blue eyes widened as she took in the majestic room as well as the lords and ladies sweeping across the dance floor, clad in their finest, the smiles on their faces speaking of utter joy that the new Season had finally begun.

Inhaling a deep breath, Alexandra willed her heart to slow down as she brushed an unsteady hand over the soft fabric of her pale blue dress, wishing her mother were here to see her during her first Season, to hold her hand and calm her jittery nerves with the usual calm that had always emanated from her all her life.

But she was not.

About a year ago, a sudden ailment had taken her from her family, plunging them all into utter darkness. And yet, life had continued, and Alexandra often recalled the promise her mother had demanded of her before she had passed.

Allow the tears to pass and reclaim your smiles.

Still, happiness was not as easy as it once had been, even with her mother's blessing, for her absence made Alexandra's heart ache painfully...even after a year.

Especially in moments like this.

"You look beautiful," her father whispered, his grey eyes shining as he looked at her. "Your mother would have been very proud."

"Thank you, Father." Blinking, Alexandra did her best to dispel the tears that threatened. Still, the lump in her throat remained.

"Don't look so sad," her brother chided from behind her before he stepped around them, a joyous smile on his face. "This is a happy occasion. Your first ball. Is this not precisely what you've always dreamed of?" William asked, his blond hair the same colour as hers.

Alexandra nodded as they proceeded forward, her gaze sweeping over the sparkling life that was now open to her. "It is," she whispered, feeling awed, and yet, oddly out of place.

"Are you trying to spot your Prince Charming?" William chuckled, teasing her as he always did.

Alexandra felt her cheeks flush and quickly glanced around to see if anyone had overheard her brother's remark. "Pray do not speak of that here," she urged him.

"Why not? Is this not the perfect place to find the man of your dreams?" Pulling her other hand through the crook of his arm, he gestured around the room at the many fine gentlemen in attendance. "Have your pick," he teased with a wink. "I'm certain not one of these gentlemen would dare refuse you."

Glancing at her father for help, Alexandra saw him roll his eyes as he usually did when brother and sister teased each other. "I shall procure us a drink," he mumbled and walked off.

"How about him?" William asked, his blue eyes sparkling with mischief as he pointed at a young man with a serious frown. "Or would you object to a man who does not know the meaning of a smile?"

Gritting her teeth, Alexandra glared at her brother. "Fine, if you insist on this childish nonsense, dear brother, be aware that two can play this game." Allowing her gaze to sweep the room, Alexandra gestured toward a young lady who kept her fan firmly in front of her mouth, probably because her teeth stood a bit crooked. "What about her? Whether she smiles or not is of no importance as you would never see it. Or would that bother you?"

Throwing his head back, William laughed. "Well played, Sister."

Displeased with her failure to draw his ire, Alexandra let her hand slip from the crook of his arm and walked a few steps away. Unfortunately, William would not allow her to be rid of him that easily.

"Don't pout, dear sister," he whispered, standing behind her left shoulder. "I merely meant to distract your thoughts and make you smile." He stepped in front of her, his eyes gentle as they looked into hers. "Obviously, I've failed."

Alexandra sighed, understanding that he had meant well. "You did distract me," she admitted, returning the smile that lit up his face at her words. "However, it might be more advantageous for both of us if we tried to spy a good match for each other, would you not agree?"

William nodded. "That does sound indeed far more promising. Shall we then?"

"We shall."

Standing shoulder to shoulder, brother and sister looked around the ballroom, hoping to spot a young lady as well as a young gentleman who would suit the other perfectly. It was no small endeavour, and they stood there quietly for a long while, unaware that their father had returned until he handed each of them a glass of punch.

"Is something wrong?" he asked when he saw their faces. "You look out of sorts. Both of you."

"It's not easy," William simply said without offering further details.

Sir John's bushy brows drew down as he looked at his children. "What is not?"

"Finding a spouse," Alexandra offered when her gaze fell on a lovely young woman she had met the other day at the British Museum.

"I should think not," Sir John mumbled, coming to stand next to his daughter, his eyes gazing out at the ballroom as well.

Touching her brother's arm, Alexandra leaned closer, indicating the dark-haired beauty across the room. "That over there is Lady Agnes," she whispered, noticing the slight cringe on her brother's face before he turned to look. "I know her name is far from promising, but she has a very sweet temper and she is-"

"Beautiful," her brother whispered, a touch of awe in his voice that made Alexandra look up at him.

"You seem quite taken with her," she observed, a teasing gleam in her eyes. "Shall I introduce you?"

William swallowed, and despite his best efforts, a touch of red appeared on his face. "Allow me to finish my drink first," he mumbled, unable to tear his eyes from Lady Agnes.

Alexandra chuckled, delighted with her brother's sudden reaction and the thought that it had been her who had possibly just now found the woman of his dreams for him. It was indeed a magical night full of possibilities.

Strolling across the room a few moments later, Alexandra made the introductions, and before long, she could not help but congratulate herself for her brother and Lady Agnes seemed to have forgotten everyone else in the room.

Alexandra sighed, turning her gaze from the love-struck couple and toward the gathered gentlemen. Now that she had found a charming lady for her brother, where was *her* Prince Charming?

FRANCE, 1789

"Father, you are aware that I've been sailing my whole life, *n'est-ce pas?*" Antoine asked, raking a frustrated hand through his dark hair as he stared at his father.

"*Naturellement*," his father, Hubert Duret, replied, shrugging his shoulders. Then he continued down the starboard side of the *Destinée*, which lay moored in the harbour, his gaze sweeping over the rigging and up to the crow's nest before he turned back to look at his son. "However, up until today, you have not been the captain. There is a difference."

"I am aware of that," Antoine replied, doing his best to conceal his annoyance with his father's rather unexpected lecture. "Still, I do not see why you would feel the need to instruct me on the matter. If you have no faith in my abilities, I wonder why you agreed to hand over the *Destinée* in the first place."

Sighing, his father crossed his arms in front of his chest and leaned back against the rail, his gaze focused on the distant horizon. "I know that you're a fine young man, my son." For a moment, his father shifted his gaze to look at him. "I've seen what a fine sailor you are and how you keep your wits about you in a crisis. You act with care and caution, and you understand the responsibilities that go with being the captain of a ship, of a crew." Nodding, he met his son's gaze once more, his grey eyes clear and sincere. "I do not doubt you, Antoine. All I wish to do is prepare you, guide you, see you happy."

Feeling himself relax, Antoine settled back against the rail beside his father. "You taught me well," he said, remembering the first time his father had taken him out, "and I thank you for it. Without your guiding hand, I would not have become the man I am today."

His father smiled, turning gentle eyes to him. "Your words are music to a father's ears." He chuckled when Antoine dropped his gaze. "Do not pretend you are not as affected by this change as I am," his father exclaimed, pushing off from the rail and coming to stand in front of his son. "Life will be different after today, and although I am certain I've taught you all there is to know about navigating the sea, I fear I might have neglected another matter. One of equal or even higher importance."

Antoine frowned, unable to think of anything more important than setting sail.

"Family," his father replied. "Love. Marriage."

Antoine rolled his eyes. "You're wrong, Father. You've said quite a lot on the matter, and I had hoped that you had finally understood that we are different in that regard." Straightening, he met his father's gaze. "I love my family, Mother and you. Alain and little Henri. Everyone. However, I myself am not a man made for marriage."

Grinning, his father chuckled. "Only a man who hasn't yet met his other half would speak thus."

Antoine shook his head. "You speak as though it is inevitable but-"

"It is," his father interrupted, and Antoine could not deny that the old man's eyes shone with a conviction he had rarely seen on his face.

"Perhaps for some people," Antoine replied, hoping to placate his father. "However, I would never choose love over the sea. This," he pointed at the distant horizon, "is my home. This is who I am. Nothing will ever change that."

An indulgent look came to his father's grey eyes as though Antoine was nothing but a child ignorant of the ways of the world. "Whether you choose love or not does not matter," his father spoke ominously. "When it finds you, there will be no choice."

Antoine sighed, understanding that no matter what he said his father would not be dissuaded from his opinion. "Can we agree to disagree on this?"

Again, his father chuckled. "If you wish," he said, that knowing look back in his eyes. "But promise me one thing."

Relenting, Antoine nodded.

"When you find her," his father said, his gaze intent on his son's, "do not hesitate. Do not fear. Do not run. For if you do, you will regret it for the rest of your life."

Swallowing, Antoine nodded once more. "I promise." Although he did not believe as his father did, Antoine could see that his father only meant well, that he was convinced that Antoine would inevitably find himself in love and wanted him to be prepared.

Certainly, there was nothing wrong with being prepared...even if that situation one had prepared oneself for would never arise. If it gave his father peace of mind, Antoine would promise to do as he was bid. Still, in his heart, he knew that nothing and no one could ever replace the sea, the feeling of the wind on his face, the sense of freedom when the *Destinée* cut through the waves.

Anyone who ever contemplated giving this up was a fool.

After all, there was no greater feeling than the feeling of absolute freedom, was there?

Chapter Two

AN IMPOSSIBLE CHOICE

Watching her brother in love only reminded Alexandra that she was not.

Certainly, she had spent the past few weeks dancing through ballrooms and attending society teas, accepting rides through Hyde Park and strolling through the British Museum on rainy days. She had met countless young and not so young gentlemen, who paid her compliments and asked for the next dance. And while they all seemed quite amiable-some more than others-none managed to put that utterly transfixed smile on her face she saw whenever Lady Agnes looked at her brother.

It was utterly frustrating.

You're a dreamer, her mother's voice echoed in her head. *And while there's nothing wrong with dreams, dreamers often tend to find themselves facing disappointment.*

Had her mother been right? Would her hopes for a fairy tale romance be disappointed because she had expectations that were too high? Did Lady Agnes feel no more strongly for her brother than Alexandra felt for Mr. Bancroft? Was it simply that Lady Agnes was perfectly satisfied with the feelings she experienced? And was Alexandra asking for too much?

Accepting Mr. Bancroft's request for the next dance, Alexandra willed herself to make more of an effort. "The music is wonderful, is it not?" she said, smiling up at him, admiring the sparkling green of his eyes. Eyes that looked down at her with kindness and affection. Eyes that looked deep into hers as though they wished to know her true self. Eyes that ought to make her feel weak in the knees.

Unfortunately, they did not.

"It is indeed," he replied, his hand grasping hers when the steps led them back together. "It is a truly enchanted evening."

Alexandra nodded, wishing his words were true.

His fingers brushed over hers, and Alexandra wondered if she would have felt at least a little jolt had her gloves not been in the way. Had his skin touched hers, would she have felt something?

Deep down, Alexandra doubted it very much.

Throughout the rest of the evening, Mr. Bancroft asked her to dance once more and constantly found a reason to venture near her, offering her a drink, asking if she wanted to stroll out onto the terrace. He was very attentive, proper in his manners and never failed to speak to her kindly. He treated her with respect and listened when she talked, and yet, Alexandra could not claim that she longed for his presence whenever she did not find him nearby.

Almost desperately, Alexandra wished she would lose her heart to him, but it was no use. Her heart remained where it was, utterly unaffected by the young man's good looks and charming smiles.

Weeks passed, and Alexandra came to realise that all she felt was excitement for something she did not have. By all accounts, she seemed in love with the idea of being in love. However, no man could measure up to the ideal she had pictured in her mind ever since she had been a little girl.

The flowers in their garden were in full blossom when Alexandra was called into her father's study one afternoon. Settling into one of the armchairs facing his desk, she looked at him expectantly. "What is this about, Father? I admit the look on your face is a bit alarming."

Closing his eyes, he sighed, and Alexandra felt a cold shiver run down her back. What had happened? Was his health declining?

"I'm afraid this week has not been kind to us," her father began, his hands unable to remain still as he began to sort through papers on his desk. "I've been made aware that Lady Agnes's father does not favour your brother's suit."

Alexandra sucked in a sharp breath. "That is awful. Can he not see how deeply in love they are?"

"I'm afraid that is of no importance to him," her father replied, a hint of guilt in his eyes that made Alexandra wonder what else he had to tell her.

Waiting, she sat back, watching her father, not needing to ask what objections Lady Agnes's father might have. Although William was a dashing, young man with impeccable manners, he was only a baronet's son and possessed no great fortune to speak of. Therefore, it was not far-fetched that an earl had higher hopes for his daughter, certain she could find a *better* match.

At least in his opinion.

Probably not in hers.

"Is there nothing we can do?" Alexandra finally asked, knowing that there was not. Still, her heart ached for the two young people, and she cursed the world for bringing them together only to tear them apart again. More and more, Alexandra came to realise that the real world had very little to do with the fairy tales of her childhood.

Had it only been a few months since she had begun her first season with such high hopes? Such optimism? How had this happened?

"I was given to understand," her father began, his gaze firmly fixed on his desk, "that...eh..."

Frowning, Alexandra stared at her father. Never in her life had she seen him groping for words like this, and her body grew cold with dread. Whatever he had to say had to be truly horrible!

"In fact, it was Lady Agnes who told your brother of her father's concern with our family's...lack of station." Clearing his throat, her father shuffled papers from left to right. "In her opinion, the earl might be persuaded to grant his permission if our family were to... marry into a higher circle."

Alexandra was very much aware of the fact that her father refused to look at her, and although her heart raced with something akin to panic, her mind concluded quite reasonably that her father was likely speaking about her. "Father," Alexandra said, her voice feeble as she spoke, "may I ask you to speak plainly? What is it that you would ask of me?"

At her direct question, her father's head snapped up, and she could see pain in his grey eyes. "I'm sorry, my child," he said, his voice close to breaking. "It is not fair for me to speak to you about this, but you are your brother's only chance."

Alexandra swallowed. "How?"

"A few days ago," her father began, his hands gripping the table top, "I received a marriage proposal for you." Alexandra started to feel faint. "If you were to accept him, it would in all likelihood facilitate your brother's suit."

Closing her eyes, Alexandra inhaled a deep breath. Whoever it was, she already knew that she did not wish to accept it as there was no one who had ever tempted her heart. Meeting her father's eyes once more, she finally asked, "Who is it?"

"Viscount Silcox."

Alexandra frowned, unable to recall the gentleman her father spoke of.

"He asked you to dance at Lord Northey's ball a fortnight ago," her father reminded her, his jaw tense as he spoke. "Right after Mr. Bancroft returned you to my side."

Alexandra's eyes opened wide as recognition dawned and she could finally picture the gentleman's face. However, recognition was immediately followed by an almost desperate desire to escape that union. "I cannot," she whispered almost breathless, shaking her head as though it could undo the proposal. "He's...I mean...he's..."

"Old enough to be your father?"

Alexandra flinched at the anger in her father's voice. Still, when her eyes met his, she saw nothing but pain and regret.

"Of course not," he said, rising from his chair and coming to stand beside her. Then he held out his hands and helped her to her feet. "I will not force you to accept him," he said, his gaze holding hers as her hands rested securely in his own. "However, I had to ask."

Searching his face, Alexandra finally realised the impossible situation her father found himself in. Although he knew very well that asking her to marry Lord Silcox would lead to her unhappiness, protecting her from such a union would rob his son of the woman he loved. No matter what he did, one of his beloved children would suffer.

In that moment, Alexandra knew that she had no choice after all. Still, she clutched at straws. "He is the only one who's asked?"

Meeting his daughter's gaze, Sir John swallowed. "You cannot," he whispered, realising what she was about to say. "You do not care for him. You-"

"Neither do I care for another," Alexandra replied, surprised to feel tears rolling down her cheeks as the possibilities she had longed for only months ago were suddenly ripped from her grasp. "William loves her." Holding her father's gaze, Alexandra nodded, urging him to understand. "I've dreamed of the way they feel about one another, and yet, I have not found it."

"It's been one season," her father reasoned. "Give yourself time. I-"

"No."

At the determination in Alexandra's voice, her father quieted, his sad eyes holding hers.

"If I wait, her father will marry her to another and then she will be lost to William." Wiping away the tears that wet her cheeks, Alexandra inhaled a fortifying breath. "My heart, however, is in no danger."

"What about your dreams?" her father asked, the look on his face one of emotions torn between relief and dread. "Your hopes?"

"Dreamers often find themselves facing disappointment," she whispered, repeating her mother's words.

Instantly, her father shook his head, his hands grasping her by the arms. "That is not what she meant. She would never want you to sacrifice-"

"Wouldn't she? Perhaps not, but how can you expect me to stand by and watch my brother lose the love of his life? He'd never speak to me again. Not because he'd hold it against me-I know he wouldn't-but because whenever he'd look at me, all he'd see would be his lost chance." Again, Alexandra shook her head. "No, if I can ensure his happiness, I must not hesitate. After all, he would do the same for me."

For a long time, her father looked down at her with sad eyes, and she could see the desire on his face to dissuade her from her chosen path. Still, he could not, and it tore him apart.

"Do not worry, Father," Alexandra said, trying her best to hold her head high and appear certain in the choice she had so unexpectedly made only a moment ago. "Perhaps some dreams are destined to remain mere dreams. After all, we cannot all have our fairy tale ending, can we?" She inhaled another fortifying breath, feeling her resolve strengthen with each moment she settled into her new life. "Perhaps this is a blessing in disguise. What if I were to hold on to the dream of my Prince Charming? What if I would never find him? I'd die an old maid with no family of my own. At least, this way part of my dream will come true. I'll have children. I'll be a mother." A soft smile tugged on the corners of her mouth. "That'll bring me joy."

Her father's hands tightened on hers. "I would ask you to sleep on it, dear child." When Alexandra opened her mouth to object, he shook his head. "No, you will sleep on it. Give yourself one day to weigh your options and decide what it is you're willing to give up. You owe yourself that."

Alexandra nodded. "As you wish."

Inhaling a slow breath, her father pulled her into his arms. "I'm so sorry, my dear," he mumbled into her hair. "I wish I could see you both happy."

Clinging to her father, Alexandra allowed her tears to run freely, determined that they would be the last ones she would shed. After today, she would not cry for a life that was never meant to be. She was not a child any longer, and fairy tales had no place in the world of a grown woman. She would make do with what she had, and she would find as much happiness as she could.

That, Alexandra vowed as she finally let go of her hopes for a man she had dreamed of all her life.

After all, was it not obvious that he did not exist?

Chapter Three

DESTINY

Returning to the harbour with a merchant vessel in tow, Antoine felt his chest swell with pride as he stood on deck, his eyes sweeping over his family as they stood by the docks, waving and smiling, welcoming him back home. Apparently, his ship had been spotted upon approach-most likely by his wayward nephew Henri.

Ever since his mother had died a year ago, the boy had been running wild with no sense of discipline or direction as his father had been all but broken by the loss of his wife. Alain could barely manage to keep himself from drowning his pain in alcohol before the day was out, let alone rein in a boy of seven years who spent his days resisting any form of control.

Returning his family's greeting, Antoine barked a few orders, watching with satisfaction as his crew skilfully moored both ships at the docks, securing the sails and then lowering the gangplank. Before he could set foot on land though, Henri sprinted up the gangplank, green eyes wide as he lifted his head and surveyed the large ship with a deep sense of childish awe.

At the sight, Antoine felt a jolt in his heart as a memory resurfaced. A memory he had not thought about in a long time. Still, as he looked at his nephew and saw the fascination and longing on his little, dirt-stained face, Antoine remembered how he himself had once lost his heart to the sea and the adventures it promised. Was Henri a born sailor as well? Did he favour his uncle instead of his father, who could not even bring himself to set foot on a moored ship for fear of seasickness?

"I see you've been successful," Antoine's father said as he stepped on deck, his old eyes sweeping over his former ship. "How does it feel to be captain?"

Turning his attention from his nephew to his father, Antoine sighed, "It is a feeling like no other."

"Then it is everything you hoped it would be?"

Antoine nodded. "That and more." Then he gestured to his quartermaster to begin and have the crew unload the merchant ship's cargo before nodding to his mother, who stood with the rest of his large family on the docks, her watchful eyes narrowed as she looked from him to her husband.

"Did you dock anywhere?" Hubert asked, his gaze distant as he looked up at the crow's nest. Still, there was a slight note of excited curiosity in his voice that made Antoine wonder what this was about.

"Not this time," he replied, eyeing his father carefully. "Why do you ask?"

Hubert smiled, finally meeting his son's gaze. "Oh, an old man can be curious, *n'est-ce pas?*"

"Curious about what?"

Hubert shrugged, strolling down the main deck, gently running his weathered hand over the handrail. "I still remember the day I met your mother."

Antoine sighed, finally realising what his father was dying to know. "To put your mind at ease," he spoke before his father could continue his stroll down memory lane, "I have not met a woman, and I do not intend to."

His father chuckled, "Neither did I."

Antoine rolled his eyes, trying his best to control the annoyance in his heart. "I am not you, and I had hoped you'd come to accept that."

Hubert scoffed, "I know that you're not me. I never said you were, but that does not mean I wish to see you unhappy."

"I'm not unhappy," Antoine insisted, glancing at Henri who had ventured over to the merchant vessel and was currently darting back and forth on deck as his uncle's crew did their best to unload the cargo without tripping over the boy.

"Neither are you happy," Hubert observed, shaking his head at his grandson before turning his grey eyes back to his son. "You might think that you are, but only someone who has never loved can truly believe so."

Running his hand through his hair, Antoine sighed, "What do you want me to say? Is there anything I can say that would stop this nonsense? That would put your mind at ease?"

"I don't want you to say anything," Hubert insisted. "I only wish you would stop running away from the fact that there is more to life than being out at sea. Believe me, the older you get the more you start to realise that family is all that matters." He sighed, "I simply do not wish for you to wake up one day and find yourself completely and utterly alone."

Holding his father's gaze, Antoine tried to make himself heard. "I have a family in case you've failed to notice. I am not alone. I don't know what else to tell you."

Again, Hubert sighed, and this time Antoine thought to see a hint of resignation in his grey eyes. "Well, then let me ask you for a favour."

Antoine tensed. "A favour? Does it have to do with marriage?"

His father chuckled, "Don't be so negative, my son." Grinning, he shook his head, and his gaze returned to his grandson as he climbed the rigging to the merchant ship's crow's nest. "This is about Henri."

Following his father's gaze, Antoine frowned. "What about him?"

"He needs direction," Hubert sighed, turning to look at Antoine. "He needs a strong hand, and above all, he needs his hands and his mind occupied." He shook his head. "Alain is in no state to be the father Henri needs right now. He barely gets through the day."

Antoine felt a sense of dread crawl up his spine. "Still?" he asked. "Hasn't it been a year since...?"

Hubert met his son's gaze, a touch of incredulity in his eyes. "This is not a cold that can be cured with a little bed rest, my son," Hubert all but reprimanded him. "Your brother had his heart ripped from his chest and is now forced to continue without it. Not even I can imagine what that must feel like as my own still beats steadily in my old chest."

"I'm sorry," Antoine mumbled, seeing the depth of his father's emotions but unable to understand their full meaning. "What can I do?"

Hubert met his gaze. "Take him with you."

"What?" Antoine's mouth fell open as he stared at his father. Then his gaze drifted to Henri, who currently dangled from the rigging, his feet flailing around as he tried to regain his footing. "Why?"

"Because it's what he needs," Hubert explained, chuckling when he saw his grandson clutch the rigging with arms and legs, his head bright red from fear of falling. "More than that, it is what he wants."

Antoine shook his head, trying to think of a way to make his father see reason without outright refusing to help his family in a time of need. Still, he could not imagine taking the boy out to sea. That was the kind of responsibility he had never wanted. Some men, like his father, might dream of a wife and children. However, Antoine was not one of them, and he feared he would only disappoint his family if he were to agree. What if something were to happen to Henri? After all, the sea was unpredictable. "It wouldn't be safe," he finally said, not liking the way his father's eyes narrowed in suspicion.

"Are you the captain or not?" Hubert asked, a challenge in his grey eyes.

Antoine gritted his teeth. "The captain of a capable crew, yes. Anyone who cannot pull his weight has no place on a ship."

"He will," Hubert replied. "The boy is eager to learn. All he needs is a guiding hand."

Antoine closed his eyes and sighed, knowing only too well that his father's mind could not be changed once he decided on something. "What does Alain say?" he asked, grasping at straws.

"He'll miss him," Hubert said, "but he knows it'll be for the best. Even in his own misery, he can see that he is no father for the boy at present." He stepped up to his son and met his gaze. "Now, it's up to us. We need to step up. We're family. We take care of our own."

Resigned, Antoine nodded. "We do." Then he sighed and glanced across at the other ship where Henri stood at the helm, his little hands wrapped around the wheel as he glanced across the deck toward the horizon. "I'm sure he'll do fine," Antoine mumbled, surprised to realise that he believed his words.

Perhaps Henri was not a lost cause and taking him on board might not prove to be the disaster it had first seemed. Perhaps the boy could be taught and all he needed was a little guidance. Perhaps his father was right.

"Thank you, my son," Hubert said, clasping a hand on Antoine's shoulder. "I'm proud of the man you've become, never doubt that." A teasing grin tugged on the corners of his mouth. "Still, a father can never resist the urge to impart some of his hard-won wisdom."

Antoine chuckled, knowing how fortunate he was to have a father who respected him. "I'll always be at a disadvantage then, *n'est-ce pas?* You'll always know more, and I'll always be doomed to listen."

Hubert grinned. "I'm afraid so, my son, which is why sons become fathers. It's the circle of life. Don't close yourself to it."

Antoine smiled, impressed by his father's ability to always come back to this topic. Perhaps he ought to marry after all to put an end to this endless discussion. Still, if his father were to have only the slightest inkling that the woman he had chosen was not *the one*, his other half, Antoine would never hear the end of it.

If only such a woman could be found anywhere!

Chapter Four

NOTHING IS SET IN STONE

Aware that she was far from a radiant bride, Alexandra tried her best to smile.

Seated beside her new husband, she glanced around the room at the many guests who had joined them for this festive celebration. Around the long table sat friends and family of the bride and groom, chatting happily and enjoying the beautiful morning.

Even Lord Silcox, Alexandra's new husband of barely an hour, sat leisurely in his seat, a glass in his hand as he accepted his friends' well wishes. Occasionally, his gaze would turn to her, and Alexandra would force another smile onto her face, doing her best to ignore the way his eyes travelled over her body, lingering in places that made her feel sick to her stomach. Still, he was her husband, and he had every right to look at her so intimately, did he not?

When the breakfast ended and people strolled around the room, standing here and there in little groups to continue their lively conversations, Alexandra found William beside her, taking her hand and leading her away. His eyes were downcast, and she could tell from the way his shoulders tensed and his hand clenched around hers how angry he was.

Once they had slipped out of the room and onto the terrace, he turned to her, his usually gentle eyes alight with a burning rage. "I should never have let you do this," he hissed, raking his hands through his blond hair. "How could I have done this?" He shook his head in disbelief. "I stood by and watched it happen. I didn't...I should've..."

Stepping forward, Alexandra drew his hands into hers, holding them tightly. "This was my choice," she said, surprised by the strength in her voice. "Do you hear me? This was my choice. Not yours."

The anger in his eyes vanished, replaced by an all-consuming sadness. "But you did it for me," he objected, his voice suddenly feeble and without strength.

Alexandra sighed, alarmed by the way her own resolve seemed to waver at the sight of her brother's resigned face. Gritting her teeth, she willed herself to hold her head high. She would not cower. She would not weep. She was not a victim. *This* had been *her* choice. "No, I did it for myself."

A deep frown came to her brother's face before his gaze drifted to the French doors through which Alexandra's husband was visible as he spoke with his old friend, Lord Dowling. "Don't tell me you care for him," her brother demanded, his grip tightening on her hands. "You cannot fool me to believe that-"

"I'm not," Alexandra interrupted. "I will not pretend that I chose him because I feel love for him or affection." A cold shiver ran down her back, and she failed to conceal it.

Instantly, William's eyes narrowed. "Then don't tell me you did this for yourself. You-"

"I did do it for myself," Alexandra insisted, afraid to relinquish her hold on this conversation, afraid to listen to what her brother had to say. "But I did it for other reasons."

His jaw clenched, but Alexandra did not miss the small spark of hope she had seen in his eyes.

"I made this choice for two reasons," Alexandra said, her insistent gaze urging him to believe her. "I will not deny that one of those reasons was to see you happy." William's mouth flew open, but Alexandra silenced him. "How can you blame me for wanting to see you happy? You're my brother, and your pain is my pain. You've found a woman you love, and the two of you deserve to be happy." Swallowing, Alexandra shook her head. "I've never even felt a flicker of what I see in her eyes when she looks at you. Never. Not once. I've always dreamed of the kind of love I see between you two, but I've come to realise that I will never find it. Perhaps I simply cannot love that way. Perhaps-"

"You've had one season, Sister," William objected. "You've not given yourself enough time. You should have-"

Alexandra shook her head. "Lady Agnes is not the first woman you have...felt something for, is she?"

William swallowed. "No, but-"

"But she's different," Alexandra finished. "What you feel for her does not compare to other feelings you've had before."

Her brother nodded in agreement, a hint of confusion in his eyes. "What are you trying to say?"

"I'm trying to say," Alexandra replied, blinking back tears of frustration, "that it's not simply that I've not fallen in love, I've never felt... anything." She swallowed. "When a handsome and kind gentleman asks me to dance, I should feel...something, shouldn't I? A small spark. A slight tingle of excitement." Swallowing, she shook her head. "But nothing. I've never felt anything. Perhaps I'm not capable of these emotions."

"That's nonsense!"

"How do you know?" Alexandra demanded. "How do you know I would not simply sit around waiting for the rest of my life, hoping for something that can never be? How do you know?" Determined, she shook her head. "I cannot risk that because there is something else I want. Something else I dream of."

William frowned. "What?"

A soft smile tugged on Alexandra's lips. "I want to be a mother," she whispered. "I want children. I want to hold them in my arms and rock them to sleep. I want to cuddle them close and read them stories. I want to dry their tears and assure them that all will be well again. I want all that. I want to be like Mother. But if I spend the rest of my life waiting, I'll never have that either."

Pulling her into his arms, William held her close. "You will be a wonderful mother, Alexandra. I have no doubt." He pulled back, and his eyes met hers. "But I cannot help but feel guilty for the choice I forced on you. I-"

"Perhaps it's a blessing in disguise," Alexandra whispered, unable to bear that look of anguish in his eyes. "Perhaps it was exactly what I needed to realise the truth. Perhaps without it, I would have spent my whole life waiting, realising only too late that my dream would never come true." A soft smile came to her face. "So, in truth, it was you who opened my eyes, and I want to thank you for it."

Nodding, William stepped back, and although the look in his eyes was far from happy, Alexandra detected a touch of relief in the way he stood before her. Over time, he would come to forgive himself and be truly happy. That was exactly what she wanted for him, what he deserved.

"Have you spoken to your beloved?" Alexandra asked, determined to change the topic. "Is there any news from her father?"

William sighed, "He has given his blessing."

Joy surged through Alexandra as she stared at her brother. "Oh, William, that is wonderful!" She flung herself into his arms. "I'm so happy for you. No one deserves it more."

"You deserve it more," William whispered. "You, dear sister."

Stepping back, Alexandra smiled at him. "You have such a kind heart, dear brother."

For a moment, he looked at her, his eyes intense as though he was wrestling with a bout of conscience. Then he pulled her close, his hand lifting her chin, so she could not look away. "Don't ever give up," he ordered, his voice harsh with determination. "Don't ever give up on your dreams. Your other half might still be out there somewhere. Perhaps he is simply...delayed." He inhaled a deep breath, his eyes burning into hers. "You might still find him. Don't give up."

Alexandra swallowed, feeling her resolve weaken, and panic began to lick at her heart. "You forget that I'm married." She had meant to say it lightly, but her voice almost broke.

"I don't care," William growled, and the hand on her chin tightened. "Nothing is set in stone. Promise me, should you ever find him, you will think only of yourself and take the same risk you so willingly have taken for me. Promise me!"

Alexandra felt her chin tremble as tears welled up in her eyes. "I promise," she whispered before her brother once more pulled her into his arms, cradling her close, offering what comfort he could.

Deep down, Alexandra knew that she would never be faced with that decision. Still, a small part of her would not relinquish the last glimmer of hope, urging her to believe that the day might come when *he* would find her.

When *he* would come to take her away.

Like in the fairy tales.

Chapter Five

POSSIBILITIES

The wind blew strong, and the sun shone brightly.

"It's a beautiful day, isn't it?" Antoine remarked, glancing down at his little nephew as he sat on the main deck of the *Destinée*, back resting against the rail, a ripped sail in his lap. Guiding the needle through the fabric, Henri groaned when he pricked his finger and a drop of blood welled up. "*Merde!*"

Antoine chuckled, and Henri cast him a hateful glare before lowering his gaze back to the task at hand. Watching his nephew, Antoine had to admit that he was impressed. Never would he have thought the boy would show such perseverance, such determination to learn, to succeed.

When Hubert had told his grandson that he was to go out to sea on the *Destinée*, Henri's eyes had gone round as plates, and for a short eternity, he had been speechless, staring at his grandfather in utter disbelief. Then excitement had bubbled over in his veins, and he had danced and cheered for hours on end, unable to sit still, wishing they could depart that very second.

Even then, Antoine had known that Henri's idea of life at sea had been a romanticised one. All he had imagined was himself standing at the helm or the bow and gazing out at sea, feeling the wind in his hair. He had thought of boarding ships, without spilling a drop of his own blood, and returning to France with glory. These dreams were normal at Henri's age. After all, he had never experienced life at sea. How was he to know the truth? And could one even know something one had never experienced oneself, but only ever been told about?

Antoine doubted it very much. After all, twenty years ago, he had faced the same reality as Henri did now when he had gone on his father's ship and realised that life as a privateer also meant diligent work and sacrifice for the good of others.

Watching his nephew, Antoine knew that Henri had come to realise his mistake. Still, the boy would not give up. As much as he cursed, he did the work assigned to him as best as he could, never once trying to shirk his responsibilities.

"I'm proud of you," Antoine said, watching the dark-haired head bob up and narrowed green eyes look into his.

"You are?" Henri asked, doubt in his voice. "Why?"

Kneeling, Antoine sat down beside his nephew. "Because you're strong and determined," he said, aware of the way Henri's shoulders drew back ever so slightly at his words. "You refuse to give in even though I am certain you wish to toss that sail overboard, *n'est-ce pas?*"

Glancing at his uncle, Henri chuckled, "What gave me away?"

Antoine laughed, "Well, let me tell you. I've never met a young man who knew as many curses as you do." He gently elbowed Henri in the side. "Life can be hard and daunting, but the most important lesson you'll ever learn is to never give up because you cannot know what awaits you beyond the horizon. And if you turn back, you never will."

Swallowing, Henri nodded. "I want to know," he whispered, his gaze sweeping out to sea where sky met water. "I want to see the world, and I want to know how to find my way around. I want you to teach me."

Antoine nodded. "I admit I've misjudged you," he said, clasping an apologetic hand on his nephew's shoulder. "I only ever saw the wayward child, unwilling or unable to control his own urges and behave as asked. But I was wrong. You have a zest for life in you, Henri, that needs to be directed at accomplishing something. And if this is what you think it should be, then I will aid you in every way I can."

A soft smile tugged on Henri's lips. "It is."

"Good." Antoine nodded, returning his nephew's smile. "Then I will teach you all you need to know. And while that includes sewing up a rip in a sail and swabbing the deck, it also means that you'll learn how to be a part of this crew, how to ready the ship for what lies ahead, how to navigate, how to spot your enemy's weaknesses, how to take advantage of them and much more." He inhaled a deep breath, his gaze steady as it searched Henri's. "Are you willing to commit your life to this? Because life out here is not a momentary fancy. It is...who you are, who you are meant to be. You need to be certain."

Henri nodded eagerly, the sail in his lap all but forgotten. "I am certain." His eyes shone like green sapphires, full of eagerness and excitement.

Antoine smiled. "Then come with me." Rising, he strode over to the rigging that led up to the crow's nest, tilted up his head, his hands cupped around his mouth, and called for Jacques to step down. Within moments, the experienced sailor climbed down the rigging like a spider in a web, moving with ease and seemingly without effort.

"Ay, Capt'n," he said when he landed on deck beside Antoine.

"Ready?" Antoine asked, grinning at his nephew, who nodded his head vehemently, his eyes shining with a deep longing. "Then up we go. But first," he pointed at his nephew's feet, "lose the shoes."

Henri chuckled, and they both removed their footwear and stored them out of the way.

Then Antoine urged his nephew to climb up onto the rail and proceed up the rigging.

At first, Henri was all excitement, and his movements were fast and without thought. However, the higher he climbed, the more unsteady the world became. The wind tore at him, moving the ropes he clung to, and he swayed in the steady breeze. Instantly, his hands clenched, and Antoine saw his body tense as the fear of falling rose in his mind and heart.

Following close behind his nephew, Antoine climbed around the boy so that they were side by side and he could look into Henri's slightly widened eyes. "The world looks different from up here, *n'est-ce pas?*"

Henri nodded as he clung to the rigging.

With his arm looped through a rung, Antoine leaned his back leisurely against the rigging, noting the surprised look that came to his nephew's gaze. "There is nothing wrong with being afraid," he told the fearful boy. "Quite on the contrary, it helps us ascertain where dangers await. Still, you must not allow your fear to paralyse you." He turned his gaze to meet Henri's. "What do you fear right now?"

Henri swallowed. "That I'd fall."

"And then?" Antoine asked. "What would happen?"

"I'd d-die," his nephew stammered as he clung even more tightly to the rigging.

Antoine chuckled, "Although I'm not saying there's no possibility of that happening, I believe it to be very unlikely. Certainly, if you fell from up high and landed on deck, you'd injure yourself severely. However, if you fell into the sea, you'd be all right if you'd know how to swim. Do you?"

Henri nodded.

"Good. Be aware of the possibilities, but don't limit them to the negative ones. What other possibilities are there?"

His nephew frowned. "That...I wouldn't fall?"

Antoine nodded. "Exactly. And what would happen then?"

Henri's gaze shifted upward. "I'd climb into the crow's nest."

"Do you want to?"

A bright smile came to his nephew's face, and some of the tension left his body.

"Be aware of the dangers," Antoine counselled, "but don't give them power over you. Face them. Stare them down. And although they will never vanish, they will retreat."

Henri nodded eagerly. Then he loosened his death grip on the ropes and relaxed his shoulders, allowing the wind to wash over him. For a moment, he even closed his eyes, and in that moment, Antoine caught a glimpse of the man Henri would be one day.

Strong. Confident. Determined.

And Antoine could not deny that he was proud. Apparently, his father had been right. Henri was meant to be on this ship, just as Antoine was.

Inhaling a deep breath, Henri opened his eyes, his gaze directed upward at the place he longed for. Then he began to climb once more. Only this time, he moved slowly and with precision, securing his footing before he moved higher. When a strong gust tugged on him, he stilled, holding tightly to the rigging. Still, the look in his eyes no longer spoke of fear, merely of caution, and before long, Henri pulled himself up and climbed into the crow's nest.

Stretching his arms into the sky, Henri cheered, his young voice drifting into the sky as he gazed out at the wide horizon before him.

Antoine joined his nephew in the tight space, resting his arms on the rim, allowing his gaze to travel as well. "It is breath-taking, *n'est-ce pas?*"

Henri nodded eagerly. "I wish I'd never have to climb down."

Antoine chuckled, "I know what you mean." Then he turned to look at Henri. "But are you afraid to climb down?"

Glancing over the rim, Henri swallowed as his gaze focused on the distant deck. Then he lifted his head and met Antoine's gaze. "A little."

Antoine nodded. "Good. Honesty will serve you. Never lie to yourself." He glanced down. "Do you think you can do it?"

The left corner of Henri's mouth quirked. "I do."

For a long while, they stood in the crow's nest, their eyes sweeping over the wide ocean as the wind tugged on their hair. Then Antoine heard his nephew sigh. "I used to beg *grandpère* to take me out so many times."

"And what did he say?"

Henri chuckled, his green eyes shifting to his uncle. "That the time would come when *you* would take me."

Shaking his head in disbelief, Antoine scoffed, once again wondering at the calm certainty his father had always possessed. A certainty that as a young boy had often made Antoine wonder if his father knew of things before they would come to pass. More than once, it had seemed as though nothing could surprise the man.

A lump settled in Antoine's throat. If his father had been right about this, what else had he seen coming? What other predictions of his would come true?

Gazing at the distant horizon, Antoine could not stop himself from wondering if somewhere out there was a woman he would lose his heart to...just as his father had said he would.

That thought was utterly terrifying.

And yet, Antoine felt his heart speed up with a sudden eagerness to find her.

Chapter Six

A SOLEMN VOW

SILCOX MANOR, NORFOLK 1790

ABOUT ONE YEAR LATER

Exhausted, Alexandra sank back into the pillows, sweat trickling down her temples as her eyes closed and her muscles relaxed.

A soft wail echoed through the room, and despite her fatigue, Alexandra felt every nerve ending in her body revive with a new purpose. Her own needs retreated, became secondary, as her mind and heart ached to soothe the little life she had brought into the world.

"It's a girl," the midwife whispered beside her. "A healthy, beautiful, little girl."

Alexandra sighed as joy flooded her heart, and she opened her eyes to gaze upon her daughter.

Gently, the midwife settled the infant into her mother's arms.

"Hello, little one," Alexandra whispered, brushing the pad of her thumb over her daughter's crinkled forehead, as she held her close against her breast, enjoying the feel of the infant's soft skin against her own. "Hush, hush, little one, I will look after you. I promise."

Humming to her daughter, Alexandra gently rocked her in her arms, her own exhaustion all but forgotten in the face of her dream come true.

Moments later, the door burst open, making not only the midwife jerk but also Alexandra as she had forgotten the world around her. At the abrupt jolt, the baby at her breast began to wail and squirm in protest.

"Is it a boy?" Lord Silcox's voice demanded as he looked from Alexandra to the midwife.

Bowing her head, the midwife took a step back. "No, my lord. It's a daughter. She's healthy and-"

"A daughter?" her husband growled, disgust in his voice as he glared at his wife as though she had thwarted him intentionally. "I wanted a son!"

"I'm sorry, my lord," Alexandra mumbled, still rocking the little life in her arms, afraid what her husband's harsh words would do to her little heart.

Gritting his teeth, her husband continued to glare at her as though he wished to punish her for her disobedience. "You will give me a son; do you hear me? I want an heir." Then he turned on his heel and stormed off, his angry footsteps echoing down the hall.

"Hush, hush, little one," Alexandra cooed to her daughter in a gentle voice. "Don't mind him. Mama is here." Feeling her daughter quiet down, Alexandra closed her eyes and once more sank back into the pillows, her body claiming its much-needed rest. Still, her arms stayed wrapped around the precious life she had longed for, and even in sleep, Alexandra was aware of her daughter's gentle breathing, the way she snuggled into her and her tiny but rapid heartbeat outrunning her own.

This truly was a dream come true.

When Alexandra awoke, the sun stood much lower in the sky, and she found herself alone in the room, her daughter still wrapped tightly in her arms. Only now, the infant began to stir, her little arms moving about. Her hands were still curled into little fists, and her face was scrunched up as though she was furious with the world. Indeed, a wail of protest rang from her little mouth, and she began to squirm.

"What do you need, little one?" Alexandra whispered, wishing the midwife was still here. "What can Mama do?" Rocking her daughter, Alexandra felt a hint of panic well up, and she had to force herself to inhale a few deep breaths to calm down.

Glancing at the bell on her bedside table, Alexandra knew that she ought to call for help, but something in her heart urged her not to. Would they not take the baby from her? Was that not how things were done in the ton? Had her husband not insisted they get a nursemaid for their child?

Nursemaid!

"Of course," Alexandra exclaimed, embarrassed that she had not thought of it before. "You're hungry, little one."

As though in answer, her daughter began to wail louder, and Alexandra reached for the bell. However, when her fingertips brushed against the cool metal, she stopped. "No, they will take you from me," she whispered down to her daughter, seeing the little girl burrow her nose against Alexandra's chest like a little dog sniffing out food.

Without a moment's hesitation, Alexandra pulled down her night-gown and put her daughter to her breast. The baby latched on immediately, and Alexandra's eyes opened wide at the unfamiliar sensation. Smiling to herself, she rested back against the pillows and gazed down at her daughter, enjoying the closeness that existed between them. For a short moment, it was as though they were the only two people in the world.

Once her daughter was satisfied, her little eyes opened, and she gazed up at Alexandra for the first time, one of her little hands curling around her mother's finger. She had a strong grip, and Alexandra loved the way her eyes shone with promise. They were a dark blue like the sea, but in the light from the window, Alexandra thought to see sparks of violet dance and sparkle like stars in the night sky.

"Violet," Alexandra whispered. "What a beautiful name." Hugging her daughter close, Alexandra smiled. Still, she could not deny that even this perfect little moment was overshadowed by apprehension. As much as she vowed to guard her daughter's happiness, Alexandra knew that her powers were limited, especially now that her father had passed on and her brother was a dedicated father himself. Never had she felt more alone than in this moment when she held her new daughter in her arms. As her husband had not even glanced at his child, Alexandra was undeniably the sole guardian of her happiness. But would she succeed? Was there any chance for her to ensure that Violet grew up to be a happy, young woman? Alexandra knew that chances were not in her favour. After all, she was a woman in a man's world, and if fate did not decide to step in, then there was very little she could do to ensure her daughter's future would be as bright as she deserved.

After all, it was her husband who had the final say.

And it was obvious that he did not care for his daughter.

All he wanted was a son.

An heir.

Alexandra prayed that she would have a son soon so that her husband might forget about the daughter he had been blessed with. Perhaps that way Violet would be safe.

After all, what other way was there?

Chapter Seven

A SILENT CALL

ABOUT SIX YEARS LATER

S tanding at the bow, his thirteen-year-old nephew by his side, Antoine gazed through his spyglass at the distant coast. The sun was setting, and dark clouds drew near. Here and there, a raindrop fell as Antoine turned to Henri. "This is Norfolk," he explained, handing the spyglass to his nephew. "There are a number of ports along the coast, and merchant ships travel up and down the Channel as well as across the North Sea to further trade."

"That's why we're here?" Henri asked, squinting as he looked through the spyglass at the cliffs rising out of the sea. "To disrupt trade?"

Antoine grinned. "Indeed, we are."

"I don't see a port," Henri observed as his gaze travelled up and down the coast. Then he stopped. "Only a large house near the cliffs."

Antoine chuckled, "You did not truly expect us to make port at any of the harbours of this coast, *n'est-ce pas?* That would be foolish indeed."

"Of course not, Uncle," Henri huffed, clearly annoyed that his uncle would think of him thus. "But should we not lay in wait near a harbour or on route to intercept a ship?"

"That sounds like a much better plan indeed," Antoine agreed, noticing the sense of pride that came to Henri's green eyes. In the past six years, the rash boy had turned into a skilled young man, who knew his way around a ship, his mind ever eager to learn. Antoine could not have hoped for more.

Rain began to fall in earnest now, and the wind picked up, howling as it surged land inward. Antoine glanced at the sky and noted a faint shimmer further out at sea where the weather was still gentler and the sky brighter. The dark clouds hung near the coast, gathering strong winds as they blocked out the last rays of the sun. Knowing how to proceed, Antoine was about to call to his man at the helm to bring the ship about and steer it back out to the open sea when...something stopped him.

Antoine did not know what it was, but his gaze was drawn back to the distant beach near a tall cliff face. A stately manor sat atop the bluff, and when Antoine pulled out his spyglass once more, he half-expected to see...

...someone.

Gritting his teeth, Antoine shook his head. This did not make any sense! Turning back toward the man at the helm, he was about to call out again when the breath caught in his throat and a wave of nausea rolled over him. He gripped the handrail, breathing in and out carefully, only to realise that the assault had already ended.

"Are you all right?" Henri asked, his dark green eyes narrowed in concern. "Should we not head back out?"

Antoine nodded, proud that Henri had estimated the correct course on his own. However, as much as he knew what he ought to do, he simply could not. Deep in his chest, Antoine felt a strange pull as though his life depended on him reaching that beach. Never in all his years had he felt anything like it, and although his mind urged him not to answer this call, Antoine could not resist.

"Steer her into the wind!" he called as he rushed across the main deck, careful not to lose his footing on the slippery boards. "We're heading for the beach."

François stared at him with narrowed eyes, his hands gripping the wheel tightly. Then he nodded, clearly surprised by his captain's order but equally determined to see them through. Leaning into the wind, François turned the wheel, steering the ship toward the coast. Instantly, the wind caught in the sails, increasing their speed, and Antoine could not help but take this as a sign. Although he was far from superstitious, it was as though fate had given him wings to speed his journey. If only he knew what he would find at its end!

"Where are we going?" Henri called above the howling of the wind. "Why are we heading toward the beach?"

Antoine shrugged his shoulders. "If only I knew," he mumbled as his father's knowing smile surfaced in his mind. Was this it?

Was it her?

Had he finally found her?

Chapter Eight

WATERS OF CHANGE

P ulling a cloak tightly around her shoulders, Alexandra started toward the door. Despite the howling wind outside, she could not remain in the house. She needed to get away even if only for a moment. She needed time to process what her husband had told her. She needed to gather her wits about her. There had to be a way. There had to be...

Wiping at her eyes, Alexandra willed her tears to stop. Then she reached for the door-a side entrance to the kitchen-knowing that the howling wind would muffle her sobs.

"Mummy, where are you going?"

Gritting her teeth, Alexandra froze, knowing that she could not leave her daughter without an explanation. Quick fingers brushed away the last remnants of tears before she turned to face Violet, a smile on her face. "I need some fresh air, my dear," she said, brushing a gentle hand over her daughter's wild curls. "Why don't you find Miss Peachum and-?"

"But I want to come with you," Violet insisted, her wide blue eyes gazing up at her with determination.

"There you are, my lady," Miss Peachum, their governess, exclaimed, hands on her hips as she looked at Violet. "I've been looking all over for you." Her warm brown eyes swept over her mistress for a split second, and Alexandra could see that the old woman understood. "Give your mother a moment alone, dear."

"But I want to go," Violet insisted, her little arms crossed about her chest as she stood her ground.

Alexandra sighed, "Then come, but you need to keep up."

Clapping her hands, Violet cheered, then allowed Miss Peachum to bundle her up. A moment later, the little girl yanked open the door and stepped outside into the darkening world. Her eyes widened as she felt the wind pull on her clothes and hair, but she bowed her head and marched on bravely.

Unable to hide a smile, Alexandra ventured after her, closely followed by Miss Peachum.

The sharp wind felt invigorating as it stung her cheeks, and Alexandra welcomed the cooling effect it had on her heated skin. Her mind and heart were in a turmoil as she followed her daughter down the path and toward the cliff top.

That morning, only moments before her husband had departed Silcox Manor to return to London and more amusing pastimes, he had informed her of an agreement he had entered with his oldest friend, Lord Dowling. According to the contract the two men had signed, Violet was to marry Lord Dowling upon turning eighteen in exchange for the release of a debt. From what Alexandra could gather, her husband had lost one of his estates in a card game to Lord Dowling and now thought to retain it by offering his daughter instead. Although Lord Dowling was at present still married-which made it even more distasteful-his wife had been ailing for years. Apparently, the man had no hope for her recovery, but was instead planning, awaiting her demise at some point down the line. Not unlike Alexandra's own husband, Lord Dowling was eager for an heir that had thus been denied him. Both men seemed to be far from fortunate in that department.

Allowing her gaze to sweep over her innocent, little girl, Alexandra felt a deep ache in her heart. Violet had such a vibrant spirit, her blue eyes lighting up with adventure whenever they ventured outdoors. She was wild and free when she ran along the cliffs or the beach below, laughter spilling from her lips as she spread her arms wide, pretending to be a bird, wishing she could take flight.

Why would her father want to cage such a wild spirit? Could he not see what it would do to her?

Alexandra sighed, reminding herself that as much as she loved her daughter, her husband had never taken even the smallest liking to her. To him, she was nothing short of a possession that he could use to his greatest advantage.

The thought of Violet married to Lord Dowling sent a shudder down Alexandra's back. Only too well did she remember her own wedding day…and everything that followed. At least, her brother had found happiness with his wife and children. Still, whenever Alexandra looked at her daughter, her brother's joy was a small comfort. After all, a mother's heart ached most urgently for her children. What was she to do? Reasoning with her husband was out of the question. He would never listen. He had haughtily informed her that this was not her decision, that this did not concern her.

How could it not? It was her child after all!

Was there anything she could do to spare her daughter the fate she herself had suffered? Anything at all?

For a long while, they wandered along the cliff face until they stopped at the highest point, sloping slightly upward. Standing in a sea of grass, Alexandra gazed toward the horizon where a darkening sky met with the black waves of the angry sea. Thunder rumbled in the distance, and there was the promise of rain in the air. Her nostrils flared as she inhaled deeply, once more enjoying the powerful wind brushing over her skin.

"Mummy, I'm tired."

Gazing down at her six-year-old daughter, Alexandra smiled and gently brushed a hand over the girl's cheek. "Would you like to return to the house?"

Violet nodded, her dark blue eyes as stormy as the sea despite the gentle smile that tugged at her lips.

Alexandra knelt, then drew her little girl into a hug. "Then go with Miss Peachum," she said, glancing over her daughter's shoulder at the stout governess that had been with them since the day Violet had been born.

Miss Peachum nodded, then held out her hand to her charge. "Let's give your mother a moment alone."

Violet stepped back, her lively blue eyes gazing into Alexandra's. "Will you come and kiss me goodnight?"

Smiling, Alexandra nodded. "Of course, I will. You have my word."

Watching her daughter walk back toward the house, her little hand resting securely in that of their devoted governess, Alexandra sighed with a hint of relief. As much as she loved her little girl, these moments when she wandered the hills and cliffs to the east of Silcox Manor after supper had become precious to her. They took her mind away, carried it across the waves and into the sky, chasing away the dreariness that was her life.

Only today, the ease she usually felt would not come. Not in its entirety.

Inhaling a deep breath of the stormy air, tasting a hint of salt on her tongue, Alexandra proceeded toward the cliff, which seemed to reach out into the sea, its rock walls falling toward the roaring waves, their sound akin to a monster awakening from its sleep. Strangely enough, the violence nature sometimes possessed, the power with which it moved the waters and flung it against the rock-hard land, always eased Alexandra's nerves. A soft smile tugged at the corners of her lips, and she felt an invisible hand guiding her onward, urging her toward the water's edge.

Carefully picking her way down the side of the hill and around the cliff top above, Alexandra followed her feet as they seemed to know exactly where she needed to go. Again, thunder rumbled in the distance, mere moments before lightening streaked the sky, cutting through the heavy, dark clouds like a gleaming sword. The wind tore at her hair as well as her cloak and skirts, and although Alexandra knew she ought to turn back, a sense of freedom, of adventure, beckoned.

As her feet came to rest on the rocky beach, Alexandra's gaze travelled to the water's edge, and longing filled her heart as she imagined the long journey it had undertaken to roll up onto the short stretch of beach to the east of Silcox Manor. If it could speak, what would it tell her of the world, of the places it had seen?

Another clap of thunder shook the earth, and Alexandra gritted her teeth, fighting the voice of reason that urged her to turn back. "I only want to touch it," she whispered, her gaze fixed on the rolling waves that licked the stony beach. "Only once."

Determined to touch the turbulent waters and feel their life's essence on her skin, Alexandra picked her way toward the black stretch of churning water. How odd, that it inspired her so whenever a storm approached. How odd, that the calm, blue sea on a sunny day never held such sway over her.

As her feet carried her onward, Alexandra felt the freezing waters seep through her shoes, chilling her skin. Still, she did not stop until the hem of her dress was soaking wet, the water whirling around her ankles. As her feet began to prick and tingle from the cold, she gathered up her skirts and then reached down to run a hand through the black water, watching the small swirls as though they held the answers to her heart's desires.

If only they could tell her what to do!

Sighing, she straightened and took a step back, her spirits sinking as she knew she must say her goodbyes and return to the life that felt like a cage. A gilded cage. But a cage nonetheless. A cage that would all too soon capture her daughter as well.

Her eyes wandered to the distant horizon one last time, and then, with a heavy heart, she urged herself to turn back.

Before she could though, strong arms seized her from behind, momentarily lifting her off her feet.

Alexandra screamed.

Chapter Nine

CROSSING PATHS

P anic spread through Alexandra's being like wild fire, and a
terrified scream tore from her lungs before a hand clamped
over her mouth. A voice spoke near her ear, hard and threat-
ening, and she felt the warmth of her captor's breath against her skin.
Still, with the wind howling around her, she could not make out what
he said, only that the rhythm of his words sounded foreign to her.
From the way he held her, she could tell that he was rather short and
stocky, and his breath on her ear sent a shiver of revulsion down her
back...not unlike her husband's.

Then he began to drag her backwards over the beach, heading
south, away from Silcox Manor.

Struggling against his hold, Alexandra could only think of the
promise she had given her little girl. Would she be able to keep it?
Would she return home that night to kiss her daughter goodnight?
What did this man want with her? And where had he come from?

"*Merde!*" he cursed as she managed to kick him in the shin.

Alexandra froze. A Frenchman! Why would a Frenchman be on a
beach in Norfolk? After all, as England and France were at war-again!
-few Frenchmen remained.

Tightening his hold on her, her captor mumbled something near her ear before she felt cold steel press against her throat, the edge of the blade nicking her skin.

Inhaling sharply, Alexandra stilled as tears came to her eyes, and she could not shake the thought of never seeing her daughter again. How foolish she had been! To wander outside in such weather! Why could she not have been grateful for the few blessings she had?

As her captor dragged her onward, Alexandra felt the pebbled ground under her feet give way to large rocks as a massive cliff face rose before her like a giant looming in the dark. Water rushed nearby, toward a large opening in the rock, pooling into a small bay in a vaulted cavern, which reminded her of a grand hall in some ancient castle. How had she not known this was here? Still, she had never wandered this far.

Venturing deeper into the cavern, Alexandra shrieked as she lost her footing on the wet rocks and her feet slid toward the water's edge, the blade at her throat digging into her skin.

Fortunately, her captor held her tightly, his footing surer than she could have hoped, and he pulled her back up onto the narrow path leading deeper into the cavern.

Forcing air into her lungs, Alexandra tried to see in the dimness of the cave. Not too far ahead, she spotted faint lights, not pale and bright like the stars shining overhead, but rather warm and red as though a torch had been lit. Then muffled voices drifted to her ears, the melody of their speech reminding her of the man who still held her clutched in his arms.

As they ventured deeper into the cavern, Alexandra could make out the ragged shape of something large hiding in the darkness. Its edges seemed to move with the lapping water as though it was dancing on the waves.

Then her captor called out, and moments later, the lights came closer, illuminating the path between them and...

Alexandra froze when she found the outline of a three-masted ship looming before her. Men carrying torches moved on deck, and two came walking down the gangplank toward them, nodding to her captor and eyeing her with undeniable interest. A hint of suspicion rested in their eyes, and yet, they exchanged a few brisk remarks, followed by a bellow of laughter. Clearly, they did not think her a threat!

Of course, she could not fault them for drawing that conclusion.

Numb with fear, Alexandra felt herself pushed toward the gangplank, her captor's arms not loosening their hold on her as he dragged her up toward the ship, calling for the captain in a loud, booming voice that echoed off the walls. Still, the storm's deafening roar almost drowned him out.

Finding herself the centre of attention, Alexandra did not know where to look as the sailors on deck watched her with the same interest as the two who had met them on their way up to the ship. Averting her gaze, Alexandra found herself staring at the wooden planks below her feet, running from left to right, forming the ship's main deck. What would they do with her?

Again, her captor's voice rang out. "*Capitaine Duret!*"

Barely a moment later, the hatch flew open and a tall, dark man stepped out onto the deck.

And then it happened.

The moment she had dreamed of ever since her mother had told her her first fairy tale.

Staring at the dark stranger, Alexandra scarcely had time to note the knee-high boots, the dark breeches and crisp, white shirt, peeking out from underneath a midnight black vest and tailcoat before her eyes met his...and the air was yanked from her lungs.

Indeed, this was not the spark she had hoped for all her life, nor was it a small tingling of excitement that ran through Alexandra's veins. No, it was a wildfire that burst to life within a second, consuming her whole.

Her knees gave way, and she felt her captor tighten his hold on her, as her head spun, and her heart ached with an acuteness she had never known before.

Could this be? Was her heart capable of these overwhelming emotions after all? Again, her brother's voice echoed in her ear as he had pleaded with her on her wedding day seven long years ago. *Don't ever give up on your dreams. Your other half might still be out there somewhere. Perhaps he is simply...delayed.*

Capitaine Duret! Who was this man? And why had he such power over her? Could he truly be her other half? The man she had hoped to find but given up on when her brother's happiness had been at stake. Still staring, Alexandra could not deny that he, too, seemed shaken to his core. Had he felt it, too? The surge of emotions as though lightning had struck?

It had to be true, for he looked as though someone had punched him in the stomach. As he stepped toward them, his dark gaze held hers as though an invisible bond connected them. The muscles in his jaw clenched to the point of breaking, and he seemed utterly shaken.

However, then he swallowed and cleared his throat, forcing his eyes away from hers, and met her captor's gaze. A few brisk words flew from his lips, and in the next moment, Alexandra felt herself fall toward the deck as her captor's arms released her.

A gasp escaped her lips as she braced herself for impact, her knees still unable to hold her, her arms hanging almost useless by her sides.

Still, there was no pain.

The moment her captor released his hold on her, Captain Duret stepped forward, his strong arms catching her as she sank toward the deck. Pulling her up, he held her tightly against him, his gaze never quite meeting hers as she looked up at him in utter shock. Again, a flurry of words flew from his mouth, sharp and commanding as his dark gaze swept over his crew.

In an instant, all eyes turned from them as the men busied themselves with tasks that needed tending. Steadily, as though the ship was not swaying on rolling waves, the men hurried across the deck, climbed the rigging and began lowering the ship's large sail to the deck, a substantial rip running down its middle.

Watching the commotion with rapt attention, Alexandra inhaled a sharp breath when Capitaine Duret's hand closed over hers, pulling her arm through the crook of his. He glanced down at her, but quickly directed his gaze back toward the stern of the ship before she could even be certain of the life-altering astonishment she had glimpsed in them. Then he guided her toward the hatch through which he had appeared only moments earlier, his feet moving with the same steadiness as his sailors did.

Climbing down a short ladder and moving down the companion-way, Alexandra found herself in what appeared to be the captain's cabin. Three large windows opened to the back of the ship, showing nothing but blackness. A cot was attached to the side of the wall, and several trunks stood along the other. In the middle of the room was a large table, maps and all kinds of nautical equipment spread out over its smooth surface.

Staggering a few steps into the room, Alexandra closed her eyes and took a deep breath, feeling her heart hammering wildly in her chest. Behind her, she could feel Captain Duret's silent presence, and a shiver went down her back.

With tense muscles-to keep on her feet despite the swaying of the ship-Alexandra turned to face her captor. Her eyes found his in an instant, and her heart jumped as though it wished to propel her into his arms.

Silent like a stone column, he stood before her, his dark gaze gliding over her face, a touch of confusion creasing his forehead as he watched her with utter bewilderment. With squared shoulders, arms linked behind his back, he took a step toward her, his gaze never leaving hers.

Alexandra swallowed, overwhelmed by the sheer presence of this man. Glancing around the room, she took a hesitant step back. "W-why are you here?" she stammered, terrified to meet his eyes, and yet, unable not to at the same time. Had she been wrong? What if her heart was deceiving her? What if this man was nothing but a lawless scoundrel? "What are you going to do with me?"

For the length of a heartbeat, his eyes flared to life, and in that moment, Alexandra feared-or hoped? -that he would seize her. Still, he remained as still as before, inhaling a slow breath before he finally spoke. "I might ask you the same, *madame*," he said, a soft French lilt to his words.

"I...I live here," she stammered, her mind slow to provide an answer as she watched his measured approach. "I went for a walk when one of your men seized me."

His eyes narrowed as he came to stand an arm's length away from her. "In this weather?"

Lifting her chin, Alexandra held his gaze. "I like the sea during a storm," she answered him, a touch of defiance in her voice. "Nevertheless, I will have y-you know that I am not accountable to you regarding my reasons to be out in s-such weather. They're mine, and mine alone."

The hint of an amused smile came to his lips, and his gaze slid over her once more as though hoping to find answers she refused to give. Then his dark eyes returned to hers, and before Alexandra knew what was happening, his right hand came forward, catching a lock of her blond tresses between his fingers.

A soft gasp escaped her lips as she stared back at him, unable to move.

"You're dressed like a lady," he observed, his gaze holding her pinned to the spot. "What is your name?"

"Alexandra." Her given name flew from her lips before she could clamp them shut, wondering why she had felt compelled to reveal it. Then she cleared her throat and forced a certain arrogance back into her eyes. After all, she was a lady. "I'm Lady Silcox," she informed him, ignoring the amused curl that had come to his lips at her faux pas. "My husband is Viscount Silcox, and I'm certain he will pay for my safe return."

Captain Duret's gaze narrowed, a daring gleam coming to it as he leaned closer. "You're certain? I admit I find that an odd choice of words for a woman who is, in fact, certain, *non?*"

Taken aback at his challenge, Alexandra squared her shoulders, running a hand through her loose hair, and thus pulling her lock out from between his fingers. "I am indeed, Captain Duret. He will pay to have me returned to him." Still, deep down, Alexandra could only hope that was true. Or did she not? What was the alternative?

"Your husband," Captain Duret continued, his gaze ever watchful, "is he a good man? Does his heart beat for you? And yours for him?"

Shocked by the boldness of his words, Alexandra could not mask the truth, her lips thinning as she clenched her jaw, unable to answer, unable to lie. Even if she did, he would know, would he not? Judging from the way his gaze seemed to study her face, he would not be fooled by a half-hearted lie.

"I see," he mumbled, and a touch of outrage came to his gaze on her behalf as though an insult to her would be to him as well.

Startled to find herself leaning toward him, Alexandra jerked her shoulders back, momentarily averting her gaze as she ran her hands over her dress, trying her best to smooth the wrinkles her capture had brought forth. "W-why are you here?" she asked once more, slowly lifting her gaze to his. "After all, you could not have known I would be walking on the beach. To collect ransom for me could not have been your motivation."

"It was not."

Her eyes held his, daring him to answer, to reveal something about himself. "Who are you?"

"My name is Antoine Duret."

Rolling her eyes, Alexandra stepped toward him, feeling suddenly empowered by the reversal of their roles. "You are very well aware, sir, that that is not what I meant."

"So, you do not care for my name?" he teased, his fingers reaching out for another stray curl of hers.

"Of course, I do, but-" Clamping her lips shut, Alexandra felt herself turn red at the triumphant gleam in his eyes. "Still, I wish to know what brought you to this beach."

Captain Duret's dark gaze shifted to the windows behind her. "The storm."

"I see. But you're French."

"Very observant of you, *madame*."

Annoyed, Alexandra lifted her hands to her sides, glaring at the elusive man before her. "What I meant was, what are you doing in these waters?" A part of her wondered if it was wise to question him so aggressively. However, deep down, Alexandra could not believe that this man was a threat to her.

To her virtue.

Her marriage vows.

Her heart.

Certainly!

But not to her life.

At her question, all humour left his eyes and they met hers with a hint of nervous anticipation as though her reaction to his answer was important to him. "We were lying in wait for English merchant vessels."

Alexandra's eyes widened. "You're a privateer?"

He inclined his head to her. "I am. Does that frighten you?"

"No." The word left her lips before she even had a chance to think it through.

At her answer, a shock wave seemed to go through him, and his jaw tensed as though he could barely hold back the emotions that so evidently played over his face. His gaze rested on hers with such an intensity, such longing, it sent Alexandra's heart into an uproar, hammering so wildly as though it wished to break free.

For a small eternity, they stood in silence, their eyes locked, their bodies unable to move.

And then the ship rocked, upending Alexandra's balance and sending her falling into his arms.

Chapter Ten

A FORK IN THE ROAD

Instinct made him move. Made him step forward. Lift his arms. And catch her in his embrace.

Holding her soft body against his own, Antoine stared down at her, seeing the same shock over their encounter in the wide eyes looking up at him. Her heart beat wildly in her chest, matching his own, and the way she clung to him made him wish this night would never end.

Dimly, he remembered the countless times his father had told him that one day he would find his other half and it would be unexpected and all-consuming. It would knock him off his feet and steal the breath from his lungs.

At the time, Antoine had not believed him.

He did now.

Still, all his life he had mocked his father's romantic notions of fate and destiny. Despite the deep love he always witnessed between his parents, he had never fancied himself a man who would tie himself to a woman with his heart and soul. And yet, as he looked down at Alexandra, he could hear his father's words echo in his mind, *An invisible bond connects you, and the closer you get to one another, the stronger the pull will become. Heed it, and you will find everything you never knew you always wanted.*

Only too clearly did Antoine remember the moment they had turned away from the storm and toward the main land. Although his instincts had told him to retreat to the south, knowing that danger lurked on English territory, he had felt a strange sense of...

He could not say. It had been a desperate need to reach this shore. As though his life depended on it. As though he had known that he would find her here.

Now, she lay in his arms, looking up at him with wide eyes that held no fear, no regret, no doubt. Only longing, and desire, and an all-consuming wish to stay like this until the end of time. Could it be true? Could this be real?

Whether it was or not, Antoine could not say. However, in that moment, he could not imagine ever letting her go again.

Tightening his hold on her, he leaned down, closing the distance between them, and captured her lips with his own.

The shock of their contact vibrated through his entire body, and he spun her around, backing her against the wall of the ship. Her arms encircled his neck, pulling her closer against him, and a soft moan escaped her lips.

Overwhelmed by emotions he had never dared dream existed, Antoine dimly recalled that she was another man's wife. Still, in that moment, he could not bring himself to care. After all, while her hand might be tied to another, her heart was his to claim.

Wrenching his lips from hers, he stared down at her beautiful face. "You feel it as well, *n'est-ce pas?*" he whispered, rejoicing in the deep flush that came to her cheeks as she nodded her head, tears streaming down her face, her eyes wide with utter shock.

Holding her wrapped in his arms, he rested his forehead against hers. "I've never retreated to an English shore," he whispered as her fingers curled into his coat as though she feared he would vanish if she did not hold on to him. "Not once. Until today."

A soft smile came to her lips, and she drew in a shaky breath.

Antoine swallowed. "Come away with me," he whispered, afraid to bare his soul...equally afraid not to. If he allowed her to leave, he was certain he would come to regret it for the rest of his life. No, he wanted her to come away with him. However, they would have to act fast as it was dangerous for them all to linger here too long. After all, this was enemy territory.

At his heart-felt request, her eyes closed, and a deep smile curled up the corners of her lips before her deep blue gaze found his once more and her face glowed with utter joy.

Euphoria seized Antoine...until a dark cloud descended upon her features.

His heart stopped as she closed her eyes and hung her head, utter resignation chasing away the joy that had been there moments before.

Antoine swallowed, an icy cold spreading through his body as though death stood behind him, waiting to claim his soul. "Do you feel bound to your husband?" Antoine asked, afraid to hear her answer. "Do you wish to return to him?"

Her gaze returned to his, and her eyes widened in such a way that the sight calmed his aching heart immediately. She did not love her husband. He could see it clearly in her eyes. Then what held her back? Was it her marriage vows? Was she the kind of woman who would rather spend the rest of her life in misery than break a vow that kept her from happiness?

"No," she whispered, her blue eyes holding his, "I do not wish to return to him." She swallowed, a touch of shame on her face. "I cannot believe I'm saying this, but it is true. I wish I could go with you."

"Then why not?" he asked, his hands wrapping around hers to keep her where she was. Would he take the choice from her if she decided to return to her husband? No, he could never do that. After all, her heart was hers to give. It could not be taken against her will. And even if, it would not be right.

Her gaze held his for a long moment, and Antoine could see that she was weighing her words. "I...I have a child," she finally whispered. "A daughter. I could never leave her."

Antoine exhaled, relieved to hear that it was not devotion or loyalty to her husband that held her back. "How old is she?" he asked, smiling down at her.

"Six," Alexandra replied, a touch of confusion in her eyes as she watched his reaction. "Her name is Violet."

"Violette," he repeated in the French pronunciation. "What a wonderful name!" Inhaling a deep breath, Antoine drew her closer into his arms, his gaze holding hers. "I would never separate a mother from her child," he whispered, knowing how fierce a parent's love could be. Despite their disagreements, his own parents had stood by his side his entire life. "Bring her along."

Dumbfounded, Alexandra stared up at the dark stranger who held her in his arms. In a matter of moments, her entire life had become unhinged. How had this happened? Had she not only an hour ago felt utter despair wash over her at the thought of her daughter's future that so closely resembled her own miserable life? Was she truly now in the arms of a French privateer, her heart full of ...did she dare call it love? -where before there had been only darkness? Was he truly asking her to leave England behind and go away with him?

Overwhelmed, Alexandra stepped from Antoine's embrace and staggered backwards, trying to keep her feet under her despite the swaying of the ship. "You cannot be serious," she mumbled as much to herself as to him. "This...this cannot be. I cannot simply leave." Lifting her gaze, she looked at him. "These things don't happen, do they?"

Antoine shrugged. "Not to me. At least not before today." He took a careful step closer, his gaze never leaving hers. "Ever since I was a little boy, my father spoke to me of finding my other half." He scoffed, "I always mocked him. I could not imagine..." His mouth closed when words failed him.

Tears clinging to her eyes, Alexandra nodded. "I've always dreamed of this, of losing my heart to another and finding the one man who would be my match. But I never did. Never have I even felt only a mild echo of the deep love I see between my brother and his wife. It made me believe that I simply could not love. Not the way they did."

Antoine nodded. Then he slowly closed the distance between them, and his arm came around her again while his other hand lifted her chin. His eyes were dark as they searched hers. "You did not marry for love...did you?"

Alexandra exhaled a sudden breath. "No," she gasped, and her jaw trembled with the memory of her husband's touch.

Antoine's eyes narrowed as he watched her.

"I never cared for him," she whispered, feeling the need to assure Antoine that what she felt for him was different, incomparable. "I never...welcomed his touch. I never enjoyed-"

"Do you welcome mine?" he asked in a low growl, a possessive hint in his eyes as he looked down at her. Still, he was asking...asking for permission, and deep down, Alexandra knew that he would respect her decision even if it were to displease him. He would not force her into compliance...not even if he had the law on his side.

In his arms, she felt safe, as safe as she had not since she had been a little girl. "I do," she breathed, straining upward to welcome his kiss.

The moment his lips claimed hers, Alexandra melted into his embrace, feeling her body hum with a desperate need to feel his touch. Never had she experienced anything like it. Never had she ever thought she would. Still, her mind whirled at the new sensations so unlike those elicited by her husband. His hands had always made her shrink away, had made her want to flee, to turn and escape his embrace.

Now, she did not feel such a desire. Quite on the contrary, Alexandra wished this night would never end. And yet, there was no way around it. It would end, and then? What ought she to do? How would she feel if she allowed him to sail away without her? The mere thought sent jolts of pain through her heart so unexpected that Alexandra knew not what to do.

Taking a step back, her eyes drifted to the windows at the back of the cabin and she tried to picture the life Antoine offered her. Instantly, her heart filled with joy, her whole body hummed with promise and she felt a deep smile curl up the corners of her mouth. In that moment, Alexandra caught sight of her own reflection in the windows across from her and a memory resurfaced.

A memory of Lady Agnes in William's arms as she gazed up at him with that love-struck look on her beautiful face.

How long had Alexandra envied her sister-in-law for experiencing that kind of love? How often had she wished she could feel it as well if only for a moment? How many times had she tried to convince herself that it was not to be?

Still, right here and now, in that very moment, Alexandra saw the same glow on her own face as she looked at her reflection that she had seen on Lady Agnes's. Could it be true? Was this the same love her brother had found? Was there any way for her to know? To be certain?

Sighing, Alexandra knew that there was not. Still, at the same time, she was certain that she would regret it for the rest of her life if she did not seize this opportunity to discover what there could be between her and Antoine. Were they destined to be a great love? She could not know that. Only the future could tell. But what if they did not have a future? What if she turned away from this chance? What if she did not take this risk?

Promise me, should you ever find him, you will think only of yourself and take the same risk you so willingly have taken for me. Promise me!

William's words, his plea for her to seize happiness should she ever find it, echoed in her ears, and all of a sudden, Alexandra knew exactly what she wanted. Still, this was no longer only about her. What about Violet? What about her daughter?

"Come with me," Antoine whispered against her lips, his arms holding her tightly. "I promise I will give you the life you deserve, you and your daughter."

Seeing the sincerity in his eyes, Alexandra sighed with joy. Still, was it selfish of her to agree? "I want to," she assured him, hoping he could see how much she did. "But I have to think of my daughter. Do I have the right to uproot her? To take her from her home? The life she was born to? The future she-?" Alexandra swallowed, and a cold shiver snaked down her back as she pictured exactly what her daughter's future would look like.

In that moment, Alexandra knew what she had to do if she wanted Violet to find love one day, to find a man like Antoine, and not be traded off to a man like Lord Dowling.

"Yes," she breathed, her hands clinging to his arms. "We will come with you."

Chapter Eleven

NOW OR NEVER

Antoine did not miss the moment Alexandra made up her mind. A sudden fear and dread sprang to her eyes and she turned to him, seeking comfort and safety.

"Yes," she whispered, her voice suddenly determined. "We will come with you."

Although joy spread through his heart, Antoine could not ignore the nagging suspicion that she had just chosen to go with him out of a reason that was not the desire to be with him. "Are you certain?" he asked, silently kicking himself for risking to lose her. "What were you...thinking just now? What was it that made you agree?"

Alexandra's face tensed. "Only this morning, my husband told me that he signed a marriage contract for Violet. He plans to marry my daughter to his oldest friend to settle a debt." A desperate fear shone in her eyes, and Antoine felt his stomach turn at the thought of an arranged marriage. Especially one like that.

"I cannot allow this to happen," Alexandra forced out through gritted teeth, anger darkening her voice. "He has never cared for her. She deserves better."

Antoine nodded solemnly. "I agree." He inhaled a deep breath, unable to keep himself from speaking his mind. "You wish to see her safe and free to make her own choice." Alexandra nodded, and a small smile came to her face. "And so, you choose the lesser of two evils."

At his words, the smile died on her lips. "The lesser of two evils?" she stammered, gawking at him in incomprehension.

Stepping back, Antoine released her, his jaw clenched as he glared at her. "I cannot fault you for wishing to protect your daughter," he said, his voice calm and yet deadly low. "Still, I can fault you for not speaking honestly. If she is the only reason you wish to come with me, then I need to know now. You cannot ask me to risk everything I am without knowing how-"

Her gaze narrowed as he spoke, and her hands settled on her hips. Then she stomped toward him. "And what of *your* honesty?" she demanded, the blue in her eyes stormy like the sea. "Have you even thought about what it means to raise another man's child when you offered to take us away? Did you simply agree for her to accompany us because you want me-?"

Mesmerised by the fierceness of her spirit, Antoine found himself reaching for her. Pulling her against him, he kissed her with the same passion he saw burning in her eyes. For a moment, she tried to resist his embrace, her hands shoving against his chest, before emotions overwhelmed her and she kissed him back with equal measure. Then she abruptly turned her head and broke their kiss. Her eyes were wide as she stared back at him, her breaths coming in shuddering gasps. "How do I know I can trust you? That I am right to put my life in your hands? My heart? If I agree, I am at your mercy. How do I know you won't betray me? Cast me aside?"

Panting, he stared into her eyes. "Can you not see that you're already holding my heart in your hands? Can you not see that the one hour we've spent together has turned my life upside down?" Grasping her chin, he lifted her head and planted a deep kiss on her lips. "Can you not see what you're doing to me?"

Barely able to catch her breath, she stared back at him. "Is this true? Are you offering your heart? Or is what you feel for me only a desire of the flesh?"

A soft chuckle rumbled in his chest, "Do you truly believe I would upend my life for a few moments of passion? Why would I offer to take you away if I could simply have my way with you right now and then set you back on shore?" At his words, a slight flush came to her cheeks and her gaze momentarily drifted to the cot behind him.

Thoroughly tempted, Antoine smiled at her, a wicked gleam in his eyes. "If you decide to come with me, there will be time for that later." Her gaze dropped from his, and she swallowed. "Look at me," he urged. "We need to be honest right now."

Once more holding his gaze, she nodded. "I agree."

"Good." Not removing his hand from her chin, nor the other from around her waist, Antoine looked down at her. "Why did you agree to come with me? For yourself or for your daughter?"

For a moment, Alexandra closed her eyes, and he could read on her face the fear of revealing what lived in her heart so openly. Still, there was no time for doubt. It was either now or never. "I felt apprehensive because of my daughter," she finally said. "I had to think about what was best for her. Not only for myself. I hope you can understand that."

Antoine nodded, remembering the utter joy that had come to her face when the question had first left his lips, and his mind calmed.

"As much as this frightens me," she admitted, "as much as a part of me urges me to be cautious, I'm afraid I cannot." The ghost of a smile tugged on the corners of her mouth. "If I ignore every doubt and uncertainty I have and only think of what I want, what I desire, what I hope for, wish for," she swallowed, stepping deeper into his embrace, "then the answer is still yes." Her fingers curled into his shirt. "You're not the reasonable choice, but the daring one. The reckless one. The one only fuelled by...love and longing. Years ago, I had such hopes, and then they were shattered, and I did not dare dream again." Shaking her head, she stared at him as though he might be a phantom. "And then I saw you, and in that moment, everything changed. You felt it, too, didn't you?"

Antoine nodded. "It felt as though something had pierced my heart, a sudden blow that threw me off my feet. Never would I have thought this possible, and I've never been so relieved to find myself in the wrong."

"Is your heart truly mine?" she asked, a joyous curl coming to her lips.

Antoine sighed, "I'm afraid so."

Gasping, she slapped his shoulder, mocking laughter spilling from her lips. "Do you truly think it wise to anger me now?"

Smiling, Antoine slipped his hand to the back of her neck, holding her close. "Slap me as much as you like, *ma chérie*. It won't change the fact that you're mine, and I will never let you go. That is a promise." Then he closed the small distance between them and kissed her the way a husband would kiss his wife.

A wife he loved with all his heart and soul.

Chapter Twelve

AN ADVENTURE BECKONS

Alexandra's heart hammered in her chest as Antoine escorted her off the ship and back down to the beach. With his arm slung around her waist, her head nestled against his shoulder, they walked back toward Silcox Manor. His hands held her tightly, and she could feel the reluctance to release her in the tension that held his muscles rigid.

When they stopped at the bottom of the small path that led up to the cliff top, Antoine pulled her into his embrace, his eyes dark as they burnt into hers. "You will hurry back as fast as you can," he whispered, his tone commanding as though his will could ensure their plan's success.

Alexandra nodded, running her hands over his arms and linking them behind his neck. Gazing up into his eyes, she wondered how she had ever lived a day without him. A few hours ago, she had not even known of his existence, and now, he was as important to her as the breath of her body. This was the kind of love she had always dreamed of. The kind of love she had feared she would never find. And she would heed her brother's advice. She would not think of all the consequences of her decision. No, she would simply act upon her heart's desire. It was a risk, yes. And yet, it did not feel like one. It felt like her life was finally beginning. After all, if the way she felt about Antoine after merely an hour or two already stole the breath from her body, how would it make her feel in the years to come?

"I wish I could go with you," Antoine whispered, and she could feel his arms tightening on her even more as he glanced upward toward the darkened manor.

"But you cannot," she replied, unable to hide the smile that came to her lips. Never had anyone felt about her the way he did. She felt precious. Special. Extraordinary.

Like one of a kind.

Like she had something to offer that no one else in the world had.

It was a heady feeling. One she never wanted to be without again.

"You must stay behind," she urged him when he held on to her tightly the moment she forced herself to step out of his embrace. "No one must see you or all will be lost. Trust me." Holding his gaze, Alexandra knew that it was not a lack of trust in her that held him back, but the dreaded notion that despite good intentions and impeccable planning, things could still go wrong.

What if her husband had returned in her absence? What if she had been discovered missing? What if she was spotted the moment she entered the house?

All these *what-if's* were not likely, and yet, they sent a shiver down her back. Her new life was so close, and seeing it slip through her fingers would surely break her heart beyond repair. Still, there was no choice. Not truly, for this new life only held wonder and happiness if her daughter was by her side.

"If you're not back in an hour," Antoine said, his voice tense and his eyes insistent as he looked at her, "I will come after you."

Almost overwhelmed by his willingness to risk his life for her, Alexandra bit her lip and merely nodded. Then after a last glance at the man she loved, she rushed up the path to Silcox Manor, praying that all would go well, and they would soon be on their way.

On their way to a new life as a family.

Glancing around the outside of the manor house, Alexandra felt her heart slow when she spotted no signs of activity. The house seemed asleep. Slipping inside the way she had left-through the kitchen entrance-Alexandra rushed up the servants' staircase, doing her utmost to walk quietly while listening for sounds of someone else approaching. Fortunately, all remained quiet.

For a moment, Alexandra glanced at the door to the nursery before she hurried into her own chamber. Quickly, she pulled a parchment from her small desk and sitting down hastily penned a few short lines to her beloved brother. Although Alexandra had come to realise that as long as Violet was with her she would not shed a tear for the life she was leaving behind, he was the one person who made her hesitate.

Despite the fact that they had drifted apart in recent years, Alexandra loved him dearly and knew that nothing but guilt kept him from visiting her more often. Still, she could not leave without a word of farewell.

Indeed, nothing is set in stone as I have come to realise tonight. Destiny has finally found me, and I will heed your advice as promised and take a risk in order to find the same happiness that you have found all those years ago. Thank you for giving me the courage to claim it.

On impulse, Alexandra did neither address nor sign the short note. After all, she could not risk it being a clue to her disappearance. William would understand. Of that, she was certain.

Still, as rational as Alexandra tried to go about her departure, tears welled up in her eyes as she folded the parchment and placed it in an envelope with shaking hands. Quickly, she reached for another sheet, blinking back tears, and penned another short letter. This one did not fill her heart with regret, but with a deep sense of relief instead. When she had finished, Alexandra addressed it to her husband and with a last sigh left it on her desk for her maid to find in the morning.

A soft knock sounded on her door, and Alexandra froze, terror crawling up her spine.

"My lady?" came Miss Peachum's whispered voice.

Exhaling in relief, Alexandra rushed to the door and then silently slid it open, her heart quickening at this most fortunate twist of fate.

The stout governess appeared in its frame, her gaze narrowed as it moved over Alexandra's sand-speckled skirts and wet hem. "Are you all right, my lady?"

Glancing down the corridor, Alexandra stepped outside, closing the door behind her. "I'm fine," she whispered, praying that the older woman would understand. "Miss Peachum, may I ask a favour of you?"

For a long moment, Miss Peachum held her gaze, speculation in the woman's eyes as though she suspected what Alexandra was about to ask before she slowly nodded her head in agreement. "Certainly, my lady."

With shaking hands, Alexandra held out the short note she had written for William. "Would you see that my brother receives this?" She swallowed. "It is for his eyes alone, and I cannot trust to send it out with the household's post. Would you do this for me?"

Once more, Miss Peachum's gaze rested on Alexandra's face, and she could see that the stout governess's mind was slowly grasping the hidden meaning of Alexandra's words. Would she deny her? Would she alert the household? Worse, her husband?

"Very well." Gently, Miss Peachum took the letter from Alexandra's trembling hands. "I promise I shall place it in his hands personally."

Exhaling a breath of relief, Alexandra momentarily closed her eyes, all tension leaving her body. "Thank you," she breathed, her voice barely audible. "Thank you so much. For everything."

"You're very welcome, my lady." A soft smile came to the older woman's face, and for a moment, Alexandra felt reminded of her mother.

"It is late," Alexandra whispered, once more blinking back tears. "You should retire. I will look in on my daughter."

"Very well, my lady."

"Thank you," Alexandra whispered once more and squeezed the woman's hand, unable to find the right words to express her gratitude.

Miss Peachum smiled, gently patting Alexandra's hand. "I hoped this day would come, but I never dared dream it would. Good luck, my lady. May you find happiness."

Touched by the governess's words, Alexandra swallowed, the

corners of her mouth curving up into a smile. "Thank you for everything."

With a last encouraging smile, Miss Peachum turned down the corridor, and Alexandra watched almost transfixed until the woman stepped into her own chamber and was lost from sight. The moment the door closed, it was as though Alexandra was given permission to move. The sudden paralysis fell from her, and she rushed to her daughter's nursery.

Casting a glance at her sleeping child, Alexandra hurried to the armoire and selected a warm dress and a heavy cloak that would ensure that her daughter stayed warm. Laying both over the back of Violet's bed, Alexandra gently sat down beside her little girl. "Violet, Sweetheart, wake up." Brushing a hand over her daughter's head and rubbing her little hands, Alexandra waited with ill-concealed impatience for her child to wake from her dream.

After what seemed like a small eternity, the girl's little mouth opened in a wide yawn, and she blinked at her mother, confusion in her dark blue eyes as she took note of the fact that it was still dark out and her mother fully dressed. "Mummy?"

"Shhh." Putting a finger to her lips, Alexandra silenced her daughter and cast an uneasy glance at the door near her back, afraid that they might be discovered at any moment.

"What's wrong, Mummy?"

Noting the hint of apprehension in her daughter's voice, Alexandra vowed that she would see to it that her child would never have reason to live a life of fear ever again. Every child deserved to feel safe and protected, and she would ensure that Violet would never doubt how much she was loved.

"Everything's fine," Alexandra whispered, brushing a gentle hand over her daughter's cheek. "We're going on a little adventure."

Violet's eyes widened in surprise. "An adventure?" She glanced at the windows. "But it's still dark."

Squeezing her daughter's hands, Alexandra smiled. "Precisely. Come, you need to get dressed." She pulled back the coverlet and reached for her daughter's dress. "But quietly," she urged. "We must not make a sound, but be as quiet as mice, do you understand?"

Alexandra prayed that her daughter would not be frightened and was relieved to see the little girl's head bob up and down in confirmation. A hint of excitement shone in Violet's eyes as she hurriedly got dressed and then allowed her mother to guide her out into the dark corridor, her little hand resting securely in Alexandra's.

Glancing into the shadows, Alexandra walked with quick steps, her daughter almost running to keep up. Down the servant staircase they went and into the deserted kitchen. All the while, Alexandra feared that someone would happen upon them and bar their way out. The little hairs in the back of her neck stood on end, and she did not dare think of what would happen if they were discovered.

Their freedom was so close. *Please!*

Once more, Alexandra unlocked the bolt on the heavy door. Then she looked down at her daughter. "Are you ready?" she asked, gently squeezing her child's hand.

"Where are we going?"

"On a ship."

"A ship?" Violet's little eyes opened wide. "You mean, like Gulliver's Travels?"

Leaning against the heavy door, Alexandra smiled at her daughter. "I do not know what awaits us, my sweet child, but I am certain that we will find happiness out there that has been denied us in here." Then she inhaled a deep breath, grunted as she pushed open the door, her strength barely a match for the powerful wind outside, and pulled her daughter out into the night toward a new life.

Chapter Thirteen

FAMILY

P acing the beach, Antoine kept his gaze fixed on the dark house. His thoughts ran rampant, and his hands curled into fists at his sides. He ought never have allowed her to go alone. What if she had been discovered? What if her husband had returned?

Minutes ticked by, and his pulse hammered in his veins as though he were sprinting down the beach, trying to outrun the waves. Then movement caught his eye, and he hid behind a large boulder, his hand on the hilt of the sword dangling at his hip. Peering around the large rock, Antoine prayed that it was Alexandra, and not someone come to search for her. However, that was unlikely, was it not? After all, the house seemed to be fast asleep, not a light in sight.

When the moonlight bounced off Alexandra's blond curls peeking out of the hooded cloak she wore, Antoine breathed a sigh of relief, and it was in that moment that he realised how much she meant to him. That she was his life, his love, the breath of his body. Panic and fear fell from him, and his heart soared high into the heavens at seeing her safe, her beautiful face looking down at a little golden-haired girl, walking beside her, the girl's little hand safely wrapped in her mother's.

Striding forward, Antoine only had eyes for the woman he loved, failing to consider the little girl, who looked anxiously at her dark surroundings. The moment he stepped into their path, a scream tore from the little girl's throat; she clung to her mother's skirts, eyes wide with fear.

For a moment, they all tensed, and Antoine glanced up at the house.

Fortunately, all remained quiet as the wind's howl had swallowed up Violet's scream, carrying it far out to sea.

Once more relief filled Antoine's heart, and he stepped up to Alexandra, his gaze seeking hers. Her eyes shone brightly in the moonlight, and a soft smile tugged on her lips as she beheld him. In answer, his own heart skipped a beat, and he reached out to draw her hand into his, his thumb gently brushing over her knuckles.

Even this short absence had been torture, and Antoine vowed he would never let her go again.

"Are you all right, *ma chérie?*" he asked, forcing his gaze from hers and once more glancing up the path they had come. "Did anyone see you?"

"I do not believe so," Alexandra whispered, her blue eyes gazing into his with the same longing he felt in his own heart. Finally, their life together was beginning, and he could not wait to spend the rest of his days with her.

"Mummy?"

The soft voice of the child reached their ears as though from far away, and Antoine blinked.

As did Alexandra. Then she looked down at her daughter lovingly, pulling her closer into her arms. "This is my daughter," she whispered, her gaze finding his once more. "Violet."

Antoine swallowed, suddenly overcome with the notion of securing this child's happiness. She seemed so small and helpless, so innocent and vulnerable. And yet, a fierceness shone in her eyes that he had only once seen before. In his nephew, Henri.

Looking up at him with her wide blue eyes-so much like her mother's-Violet stood in Alexandra's arms, and Antoine could see that there was no fear in the girl's gaze, which spoke to the trust that existed between mother and daughter.

"*Bonsoir, Violette,*" he said, smiling down at the little girl that would now be his daughter, and he knelt in front of her, his eyes finding hers. "Have you ever been on a ship?"

Violette shook her head, her blond curls swaying in the wind. "Are you a pirate?"

Antoine laughed, impressed by her courage, her blue eyes holding his without flinching. "Not quite, *ma petite*. My name is *Antoine Duret*, and I am a privateer, sailing under a French flag." He briefly looked up at Alexandra, and joy danced in his heart as he realised that there was no longer a single doubt in his heart or mind. He had finally found his family, and he could not wait to take them home. "I've come to steal your mother away. Your mother and you." Inhaling a deep breath, Antoine watched her little face. Then he held out his hand to her. "Will you come with me?"

Violette glanced up at her mother, but then she slipped her hand into his, and the feel of her little hand in his large one, humbled him. A sudden desire to protect her, to keep her safe claimed his heart. The thought that she might be harmed or hurt, that tears might fall from her eyes, that her heart might break pained him greatly, and Antoine knew that he would do everything within his power to guard her for the rest of his life.

A little voice, deep inside, whispered that the world had changed, that she was now his daughter, like a child born and placed in her father's arms. His heart opened, and a new love-one he had never experienced before-sparked into life, slowly reaching out and claiming more and more of himself. Soon, he would be hers, and he did not mind in the least. Was that not the way parents loved their children?

In that moment when they stood on the beach below Silcox Manor, Antoine began to love Violette for her mother's sake. But he had no doubt that before they would reach French soil, he would love her for her own.

Becoming a father was a strange thing.

As was life itself.

A few hours ago, he had been focused on the sea and his ship alone, and he had been convinced that there had been nothing missing from his life. And now, suddenly, he found himself in love, and a father no less, and he could not imagine ever being anything less.

Chapter Fourteen
BORN TO BE AT SEA

The sky was still dark when the tide rolled out, carrying the *Destinée* out to sea. The storm had subsided, and the dark, angry clouds moved westward as though the world smiled upon the decision that had been made that night. In the distance, dawn lurked on the horizon, and Alexandra stepped up to the bow, her eyes sweeping over the world before her.

"Are you all right?" Antoine asked, coming to stand behind her, his strong arms wrapping her in a tight embrace. "Do you have regrets?"

Alexandra could hear the apprehension in his voice and knew that they would need time to truly get to know one another. Although their hearts had instantly recognised one another as two pieces of a whole, tying them together for the rest of their days, they had both lived very different lives, and it would take some time to create one that belonged to both.

"None," Alexandra replied, her voice strong, as she felt her blood pulse in her veins. Leaning back against Antoine, she placed her hands on his, which were securely wrapped around her middle. "I'm merely saying goodbye to a life I never thought I'd ever be able to escape. A part of me can still not believe that this is real." She turned in his arms and looked up into his warm eyes. "That *you* are real. I'm afraid I might wake up any second and find myself back at Silcox Manor, our meeting only a dream conjured by my heart's desire."

A soft smile curled up his lips. His eyes, however, were serious as they looked into hers. "I'm very real," Antoine whispered, his breath brushing over her lips. "And I will never let you go." Then his mouth claimed hers, urging her to believe that what they had found was not a dream at all, but life in all its beauty. Sometimes a path was not a direct line. Sometimes it took turns and detours. Sometimes it took one a long time to travel it.

But always would it lead one to the place one ought to be.

And to the love one was destined to find.

But sometimes patience was required.

"I want to see, too," Violet demanded, her little voice tinged with anger. "Give it to me."

Alarmed, Alexandra broke the kiss and pulled back as Antoine turned to see what was going on. Looking down at the main deck, they found Violet standing beside Antoine's nephew Henri, her little hands reaching up and trying to snag the spyglass from him.

Antoine laughed, his eyes sparkling as he met Alexandra's eyes. "As fierce as her mother."

Resting her head on his shoulder, Alexandra smiled. Still, she needed to be certain that Antoine had no regrets, either. "Are you certain you don't mind her being here?" she asked, remembering the letter she had left for her husband, telling him that she'd rather take their daughter to a wet grave than see her married to an old man. Hopefully, upon reading it, he would believe them dead and not come after them.

Stepping back, Antoine lifted her chin, his dark gaze finding hers. "She is mine now, as much as she is yours, and I will not hear that man's name mentioned as her father ever again, do we agree?"

Joy filled Alexandra's heart as she nodded her head, her vision blurring by the tears that streamed down her face. "Agreed," she whispered, sinking into Antoine's embrace.

"*Merde!*" Henri cursed, annoyance clear in his voice. "Give that back!"

Brushing away her tears, Alexandra's gaze swept back to her

daughter and nephew, and a smile came to her face as she saw Violet's little hands clutching the spyglass, determined not to return it to an enraged Henri. "How did she do it?"

Antoine laughed. "I don't know, but she seems quite resourceful."

As Henri started after her, Violet turned and ran across the deck, her little feet carrying her as though she did not even notice the swaying of the ship. When there was no room left for retreat, she made to climb up the rigging, but Henri surged forward, pulling her back to safety. "I will show you how to use it if you promise not to climb up there again, all right?"

For a moment, they looked at one another, the dark-haired young man and the golden-haired little girl, who suddenly found themselves to be cousins, family. Then Violet nodded and held out the spyglass to Henri, who took it with a sigh and then began to explain to a rapturously listening Violet how it could be used.

"She seems born to be at sea," Antoine said, his eyes beaming as he looked back at her. "The same as Henri. I do not have a doubt in my heart that we were all meant to find one another. We've always been family. Apart before, and now together. Never doubt that, *ma chérie!*"

Wrapped tightly in Antoine's arms, Alexandra sighed. Never had she been this happy, her heart free to love. Never had she thought she ever would be. And then, life had taken an unexpected turn-one turn! -and everything had changed.

Alexandra's heart overflowed with happiness that she hardly knew how to contain it. Whatever the future would hold, she would be grateful for it and never take it for granted, and she would always remember what it was like to live a life of regret, a caged life, a life without choice.

Alexandra vowed that Violet would never know such a life.

She would be free to make her own choices.

It was the greatest gift Alexandra could bestow upon her.

That and a loving family.

Epilogue

As the *Destinée* approached the harbour, Antoine could see his family awaiting them at the docks. It was a clear day. The sun shone brightly, and the sky was blue. Antoine was not surprised that they had been spotted early on. Someone in his family always seemed to have an eye on the far horizon, waiting for him and Henri to return.

Only this time, they were not the only ones to come home.

Meeting Alexandra's gaze, Antoine could see a touch of nervousness in the way she brushed her hair out of her eyes. "They will love you," he whispered to her. "Do not worry. My parents will be overjoyed to meet you."

Swallowing, Alexandra nodded, then picked up their daughter, settling her on her hip, so the girl could see.

"This is where *grandpère* and *grandmère* live?" Violette asked, glancing down at Henri who stood beside them, his green eyes focused on the small crowd of people waving from the docks.

"*Oui*," he confirmed, joy dancing in his eyes as he waved back.

"Will they like me?" little Violette asked without the slightest hint of concern.

Henri nodded. "Of course, they will."

Smiling, Violette nodded, then lifted her hand and waved to her new family.

Antoine's gaze drifted from his daughter to his wife, his eyes sparkling with delight at the way the young met the world. "Don't worry," he repeated, a low chuckle in his throat. "Children have a way of knowing these things."

Sighing, Alexandra cuddled their daughter close. "I suppose you're right."

Relieved to see his wife relax, Antoine strode away to ensure that the ship made it safely to the dock. His crew scrambled to execute his commands as he stood on the quarter deck, his gaze sweeping over the treasure he had so unexpectedly found on this voyage.

Not much time had passed since they had left England, but nothing was as it had been before. Antoine loved Alexandra with a fierceness he had never thought himself capable of. He loved the way she smiled and laughed. The way she glared at him and never ducked her head even when his eyes narrowed, and he could feel anger boiling under his calm exterior. In the short time they had spent together, they had come to know each other well. They had become a family, and he could not imagine his life without his wife and child.

Violette, too, had taken to life on a ship like a fish took to the water. Trailing Henri like a shadow, she already spoke a little French and her hands were roughened from climbing the rigging. Apparently, no one-not even her watchful new cousin! -could persuade her to keep her feet on deck. After a day out at sea, Alexandra had altered a pair of spare trousers from Henri and packed up Violette's dress-torn beyond repair. The joy that shone in the girl's eyes had finally put all her mother's doubts at rest and brought a peaceful happiness to their little family.

When the ship was finally docked, Henri jumped over the rail and surged into his father's arms. Then he hugged his grandparents, their eyes wide as they glanced at Alexandra, her golden hair billowing in the wind.

Leading his wife down the gangplank, his daughter in his arms, Antoine met his father's gaze. For a moment, the older man stared at him, his eyes gliding over the two women by his son's side before meeting Antoine's gaze. Then a smile unlike any Antoine had ever seen before splitting his father's face in half, and he laughed with joy, tears misting his eyes. "*Bienvenues!*" he boomed, joy reverberating in every cell of his body as he strode forward.

Antoine had never seen him so happy, and he promised his father silently that he would find a quiet moment and thank him for never giving up on him and guiding him to the woman he never knew he had always been looking for.

"*Es-tu mon grandpère?*" Violette asked when Antoine's father came to stand before them, his laughing eyes gliding over Violette and Alexandra in the same way Violette studied him.

At her innocent perusal, his father laughed, instantly taken with the golden-haired girl. "*Mais, bien sûr.*" Then he held out his arms, and Violette flung herself at him, her little mouth talking his ear off, English and French flowing together as she told him of all she had seen and done since coming aboard the *Destinée*.

"Are you still worried?" Antoine whispered in Alexandra's ear, his arm wrapped tightly around her.

Smiling, she sighed. "Not at all. This is perfect." Tears came to her eyes as she watched Violette with her new grandparents, her aunts, her uncles and cousins and others of Antoine's extended family. "I've always wanted this for her. A family who loves her."

Drawing her into his arms, Antoine kissed her. "She will never be alone again," he whispered, his dark eyes looking into her sparkling blue ones. "And neither will you."

Whatever tomorrow would bring did not matter.

For they would face it together.

As a family.

THE END

Thank you for reading *Trapped & Liberated*!

. . .

In the next installment we meet Richard Davenport again, Viscount Ashwood, from book 3, who is known far and wide as an unfeeling and cold-hearted man. Can such a man ever fall in love?

Would a warm and caring woman like Evelyn Procten even want him?

Read a Sneak-peek

Oppressed & Empowered
The Viscount's Capable Wife

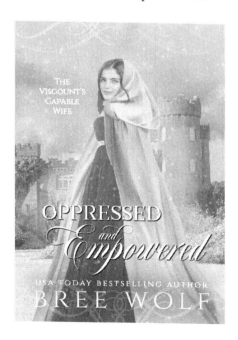

Prologue

"Richard!"

At the sound of his mother's voice, Richard Davenport, Viscount Ashwood, looked up from the letter he had been writing to his steward, his gaze fixing on the sturdy door to his study. Behind it, he heard his mother's hastened footsteps as she was no doubt hurrying down the corridor toward him at this very moment.

What on earth was going on? He wondered, rising to his feet. It was not like his mother to call out to him. In fact, never had she acted so irrationally and against proper decorum. In fact, now that he thought about it, Richard found her behaviour quite odd.

And alarming.

Opening the door, he found her all but running toward him, a sheet of paper clutched in her hand and her face flushed in such a way that his own unease grew. Although Richard knew that ladies tended to get agitated for all sorts of insignificant reasons, he also knew his mother to be a composed and level-headed woman. Never had he seen her like this.

Not since the death of his father at least.

"Richard, the most awful thing has happened," she exclaimed, her grey eyes–so much like his own–finding his. "She's done it! Now, she's done it! All is lost!"

Stepping aside, Richard escorted his mother to one of the upholstered armchairs and urged her to sit down. Then he fetched her a drink to settle her nerves, his gaze drifting to the sheet of paper she still held clutched in her left hand as though her life depended on it. "What happened?"

Downing her drink, his mother coughed, the red of her cheeks darkening. "She's gone!"

"Do you speak of Claudia?" Richard enquired, unable to think of anyone else who would put his mother into such an agitated state. As far as he knew, only his younger sister possessed that talent. Still, he had to admit that his mother's current state of distress surpassed any other reaction he had ever observed.

"She has run off!" Nodding her head vigorously, his mother stared up at him. "With William Montgomery."

Inhaling a sharp breath, Richard felt his jaw tense and his teeth grit together. "Are you certain?" he asked as a rather unfamiliar emotion claimed his heart, tensing the muscles in his body and curling his fingers into clenched fists.

His mother nodded, holding out the crumpled sheet of paper to him.

Uncurling the fingers of his right hand, Richard took it, smoothing out the paper as his eyes glided over his sister's rather child-like handwriting.

I'm away to Gretna Green to marry my dearest William. Please be happy for me as I cannot help but follow my heart. I shall see you soon.

"Headstrong fool," Richard forced out through clenched teeth, feeling a mild headache begin to form behind his left temple as it always did whenever his sister threw all caution to the wind and acted against society's rules. However, so far her indiscretions had been of minor consequence. Clearly, that was no longer the case. "Are you certain she is referring to William Montgomery?"

His mother nodded, her face suddenly pale as she leaned back in her chair. "She's been speaking of him for the past fortnight."

Richard closed his eyes.

"I've tried to counsel her," his mother continued, her voice feeble, "reminded her that he is betrothed and to a duke's daughter no less. But she would not hear of it." Closing her eyes, his mother sighed, "Still, even I would not have thought that she would do something so irresponsible." Jerking to her feet, his mother came to stand before him and placed her trembling hands on his crossed arms. "Oh, Richard, what are we to do?"

Stepping away, he turned to the door. "I shall go after her in the hopes of preventing what would be a major scandal, one she would never live down." Hastening down the corridor, he called for his butler, his mother's hastened footsteps echoing behind him. "When did she leave?"

"I do not know. I only discovered the note a moment ago. I shall go speak to her maid."

"Don't bother, Mother," Richard said before turning to his butler and instructing him to have his fastest horse readied without delay. Then he spun on his heel and faced his mother once more. "Whether she left only an hour ago or ten does not signify. There is only one reasonable course of action. Pray that I'll catch up to them before she ruins her life for good. Speak of this to no one and act as though nothing is amiss."

"Godspeed," Richard heard his mother whisper before he rushed out the door, wondering what he would do if he would be unable to prevent his sister from marrying William Montgomery, the Earl of Mowbrey's second son, a man betrothed to another, a young lady of impeccable standing, daughter to one of the most influential men in all of England.

It would indeed be a dark day.

A day that would plunge all those that followed into darkness as well.

Why could his sister not be more reasonable?

Chapter One
CONSEQUENCES

Farnworth Manor, November 1808

Five Months Later

"Richard!"

At the sound of his sister's harsh voice, Richard's hand jerked, and the quill scratched across the parchment, leaving a long, black line in its wake. Gritting his teeth, he set it aside and rose to his feet, preparing himself for yet another one of his sister's emotional outbursts.

"I need to speak to you!" Claudia announced, her voice rather shrill, as she all but threw open the door and rushed inside without bothering to knock.

On her heels, a young footman by the name of Maxwell Adams mumbled an apology as he tried to persuade her to turn back even now.

Claudia, however, completely ignored him, and Richard would not be the least bit surprised if she had not even noticed his presence. When in such an emotional state, his sister was far from observant.

"It's all right, Maxwell," Richard told the young man. "You may leave us." When the door closed behind the footman, he turned to look at his sister, her face flushed, her eyes wide and her hands resting on her sides. All signs that she was agitated...about something. "What can I do for you, my dear?" Richard asked, trying to remain calm. After all, a shouting match between the two of them would not benefit anyone, and from experience, he knew that his sister had very little self-control.

"How dare you!" she hissed, and her eyes narrowed in what Richard presumed to be accusation. "How dare you post a guard at my door? Am I a prisoner now? Not allowed to come and go as I please? Why would you–?"

"If you were to cease talking," Richard interrupted, taking a sudden step toward her, "I could actually reply to your accusation."

Pressing her lips into a thin line, his sister glared at him, her nose scrunched up in open displeasure.

"I am your brother," Richard began, hoping to discuss this like two reasonable adults. However, the way his sister rolled her eyes, he found himself losing all hope. "It is my duty to look after you. I've already failed you when you ran off to Gretna Green five months ago, and I refuse to do so again."

"You did not fail me," Claudia objected, her voice no less harsh than before. "It was my decision!"

"You cannot in all honesty claim that you have no regrets?" Richard demanded, unable to make sense of his sister. On normal days, she confused him. However, ever since he had brought her back from Gretna Green, her behaviour as well as her words baffled him.

Again, her lips thinned, and for a short moment, she was uncharacteristically silent. "Regrets or not, I do not deserve to be imprisoned in my own home. I–"

"Yes, you do," Richard objected. "You brought this on yourself, running off with a man betrothed to another. If you had indeed married, it would have been a major scandal, and if anyone were to find out," his voice dropped to a whisper, "that you're with child, you would be ruined beyond redemption. Do you not see that? Do you not understand what that means?" Shaking his head, Richard stared at his sister, wondering why she refused to see reason. After all, he only wanted what was best for her...as much as that was still possible at this point.

"I understand very well," Claudia retorted, her face twisted into a grotesque mask, making Richard wonder if she was angry or rather in pain. "I understand that you always think you know better—"

"I thought that was obvious," Richard interrupted his sister's hurried speech, his hand gesturing toward the small, as-of-yet well-concealed bump under her dress. "If you had listened to me, none of this would have happened, and you would not be under house arrest right now."

Although her jaw looked painfully clenched, Claudia ran a gentle hand absentmindedly over her midsection. "You ought not have interfered. It was not your place."

"I did not make it to Gretna Green in time if you recall," Richard reminded her, remembering his own shock at encountering young William Montgomery in the company of his elder brother on their way back to England. However, when he had discovered that his sister was not with them but had insisted on staying behind in Scotland, Richard had almost toppled over with outrage. He could not recall ever having experienced similarly strong emotions than in that moment! "It was William's brother, Lord Crowemore, who interfered and prevented his brother from marrying you." Staring at Claudia, Richard shook his head, still at a loss. "I cannot fathom what possessed you to remain in Gretna Green on your own, without a chaperone, without any kind of protection."

Crossing her arms over her chest, Claudia stared at him through narrowed eyes. "I was too disappointed in William," she replied, her voice suddenly heavy with an emotion Richard could not quite determine. "He bowed his head to his brother and abandoned me." Gritting her teeth, she shook her head defiantly. "No, nothing in the world could have persuaded me to return with them, to sit across the seat from him on the long journey back. I'd rather have died."

Rolling his eyes at his sister's foolishness as well as her tendency to be overly dramatic, Richard snapped, "And this is your reward." Again, he gestured at the small bump under her hand. "This is what your irresponsible behaviour brought you, a child in your belly from a man you cannot even name." He took a step toward her, his gaze fixed on hers, wondering if he would ever be able to understand her motivations. Richard doubted it very much! "You acted like a stubborn child, not like a well-brought up, young lady. At least, William Montgomery had the sense to recognise his mistake. You, however, allowed yourself to be inebriated and bedded by a man you did not even remember the next morning. Now, you have a price to pay, and you cannot blame anyone but yourself. Countless times I warned you, counselled you to amend your behaviour, but you would not listen. Now, your circumstances are direr than I ever would have thought possible, and if you are to have any chance at making a suitable match, then no one can know that you are with child. Do you understand me?"

Lost in his own anger, Richard had not noticed the change in his sister. Only now did he see her quivering lower lip and the way her hands clenched around her upper arms as though she feared she would break apart if she were not to hold tightly to herself. "I do understand," she mumbled, a tear sliding down her cheek. "I do understand that all you see are my mistakes."

Swallowing, Richard refused to allow the hint of guilt that rose in his heart to influence his actions. After all, he had done nothing wrong, and there was no reason for him to feel as he did. Quite on the contrary, it was his sister who ought to learn how to suppress her wayward emotions and allow reason to govern her actions. "Can you truly fault me for it?" Richard demanded. "All I am trying to do is guide your feet back onto the path set out for you, but you fight me at every step. I do not understand you; nor do I believe that I ever shall." Ignoring the paleness of his sister's cheeks, he continued, "You will stay far away from society until your child is born. Then you may return to London, and I pray that you will be able to procure a suitable husband as fast as humanly possible. I tell you honestly, that I will not mourn the day when I will no longer be responsible for your actions."

Swallowing, Claudia nodded, her pale eyes barely looking into his. "That is all I am to you," she whispered, "a responsibility that you wish you could rid yourself of. Tell me, dear brother, am I so unlovable?"

Confused by her question, Richard chose to ignore it. "Indeed, since father's passing, I am responsible for you," he stated, wondering why she would ask such a thing. "And you cannot fault me for wishing it were otherwise considering the immense effort it takes on my part to ensure that you do not ruin yourself for good." He shook his head, eyes narrowing as he watched her face, wondering if she truly did not see her actions as unreasonable. How was this possible?

For a moment, Claudia's gaze remained fixed on his, her eyes unblinking. Then, however, her lids closed once, only to open for the barest of moments before her eyes rolled up and all tension left her body. Within the blink of an eye, her body sank toward the floor, and Richard had to lunge forward to catch her before she hit the ground hard.

"Claudia," he whispered as her limp body hung in his arms, her head hanging backwards, her eyes closed. Swallowing, Richard felt his heart beat quicken as a hint of fear swept through his body. He did not care for it, not in the least, and so he pushed it aside and focused on what needed to be done.

"Maxwell!" he called, knowing that the young footman would not be far. Although he had only been in their employ a little over a year, he showed great dedication to any task given to him, which had been precisely the reason Richard had sent him to guard his sister's movements.

"Yes, my lo–" Maxwell's voice broke off as he stepped over the threshold, his eyes going wide as he watched Richard lift his unconscious sister into his arms.

"Take the carriage and fetch Dr. Procten from the village immediately," Richard instructed, settling his sister securely in his arms before striding out the door. "Tell him that it's urgent and that I ask him to attend to my sister immediately."

Without a moment's hesitation, Maxwell darted away.

Carrying his sister upstairs, Richard could not prevent his thoughts from drifting to Dr. Procten's headstrong daughter and the last time they had spoken. After his father's death, his mother had been inconsolable, taking to her bed, her cheeks white as a sheet and her eyes red-rimmed for weeks on end. It had been Evelyn Procten who had sat with his mother hour after hour, and after Lady Ashwood had finally recovered, she had voiced her delight at having had such a capable, young woman tend to her in her time of need.

Naturally, Richard had to admit that Miss Procten's presence had helped his mother. However, that was a far cry from possessing medical expertise. Nonetheless, it had been Miss Procten who—quite unnervingly—had instructed *him* to call on *her* instead of her father in case of another medical situation. Ever since her father had begun to involve her in his work, allowing her to tend to patients alongside him, she seemed to be thinking of herself as a doctor as well.

What nonsense! As though women had the necessary calm and faculty of reason to hold another's life in their hands. Looking down at his sister, Richard sighed. If that were the case, he would not be in this predicament.

Still, despite his justifiable reasons for calling on the doctor himself instead of the man's daughter, Richard could not shake the small tremble that gripped him as he thought of her deep brown eyes and the way they looked into his.

Always had she upended his rational thoughts.

And he could not allow that to happen. Not now. Not when his family needed him to make the right decisions for all of them.

No, it would be better for everyone if Miss Procten were not to return to Farnworth Manor...

...as much as his traitorous heart longed to see her.

Series Overview

LOVE'S SECOND CHANCE: TALES OF LORDS & LADIES

LOVE'S SECOND CHANCE: TALES OF DAMSELS & KNIGHTS

LOVE'S SECOND CHANCE: HIGHLAND TALES

THE WHICKERTONS IN LOVE

FORBIDDEN LOVE SERIES

HAPPY EVER REGENCY SERIES

For more information visit www.breewolf.com

About Bree

USA Today bestselling and award-winning author, Bree Wolf has always been a language enthusiast (though not a grammarian!) and is rarely found without a book in her hand or her fingers glued to a keyboard. Trying to find her way, she has taught English as a second language, traveled abroad and worked at a translation agency as well as a law firm in Ireland. She also spent loooong years obtaining a BA in English and Education and an MA in Specialized Translation while wishing she could simply be a writer. Although there is nothing simple about being a writer, her dreams have finally come true.

"A big thanks to my fairy godmother!"

Currently, Bree has found her new home in the historical romance genre, writing Regency novels and novellas. Enjoying the mix of fact and fiction, she occasionally feels like a puppet master (or mistress? Although that sounds weird!), forcing her characters into ever-new situations that will put their strength, their beliefs, their love to the test, hoping that in the end they will triumph and get the happily-ever-after we are all looking for.

If you're an avid reader, sign up for Bree's newsletter on **www.breewolf.com** as she has the tendency to simply give books away. Find out about freebies, giveaways as well as occasional advance reader copies and read before the book is even on the shelves!

Connect with Bree and stay up-to-date on new releases:

facebook.com/breewolf.novels

twitter.com/breewolf_author

instagram.com/breewolf_author

bookbub.com/authors/bree-wolf

amazon.com/Bree-Wolf/e/B00FJX27Z4

Printed in Great Britain
by Amazon

13921624R00059